An Underachiever's Diary

An Underachiever's Diary

Benjamin Anastas

PICADOR

First published 1998 by The Dial Press,
a division of Bantam Doubleday Dell Publishing Group, Inc., New York

This edition published 1999 by Picador
an imprint of Macmillan Publishers Ltd
25 Eccleston Place London SW1W 9NF
and Basingstoke

Associated companies throughout the world

ISBN 0 330 37266 1

1 3 5 7 9 8 6 4 2

A CIP catalogue record for this book is available from
the British Library.

Printed and bound in Great Britain by
Mackays of Chatham plc, Chatham, Kent

The author wishes to express his gratitude to Rhea Anastas, Joni Evans, Dede Gardener, Susan Kamil, Elena Lombardi, Carla Riccio, Sarah Rosen, and Miguel and Cynthia Ventura.

Contents

I.   *The Early Years*   1

II.   *Latency and Adolescence*   33

III.   *Adulthood for Beginners*   79

I. The Early Years

I started strong, the firstborn of identical twin boys, leading my reluctant brother out into the world by seven minutes flat, give or take a moment to suspend my infant's disbelief in the delivery room. By the time he finally emerged, feetfirst, tangled in his umbilical cord and placid in the obstetrician's forceps, I had already taken my welcome smack, wailed my way into the human race, while sure hands cut my own cord, wiped me down, and bundled me in swaddling clothes. I had a name: William, chosen by my father, who had coveted it for himself since childhood. In the turmoil of the coming years my parents would consider changing my name to Guillaume, in honor of the student protests in Paris (this was 1968), and later, after a trip to Mexico, where they toured the countryside in search of armed insurrectionists and returned with the perfect dining-room set, they toyed with calling me Guillermo. My parents were still in their Anglophilic stage when we were born, and chose a fitting name for my brother: Clive. Clive narrowly escaped becoming Claude—they were, at least, consistent—and Chico.

In their fondest dreams, then, the universe was ruled over by the Warren Supreme Court, and following the precedent of *Brown* v. *Board of Education* (1954), they believed their children would be guaranteed an equal opportunity to grow and thrive. The recent *Gideon* v. *Wainright* (1963) ruling held that, no matter how helpless or indigent, we would always have a voice in family matters. We endured no cutesy nicknames in our formative years, and wore no matching clothes. We would be ordinary brothers, they believed, just closer, and the fact that we were twins would neither limit our development nor provide unfair advantage over the silent, solitary majority. They took smug satisfaction, however, in a line from Dr. Spock's *Baby and Child Care,* which my pregnant mother had underlined in their well-thumbed paperback edition: "Twins . . . develop special strength of personality from being twins: early independence of parental attention, unusual capacity for cooperative play, great loyalty and generosity toward each other." In other words, they had high hopes for us.

What's it like to be a twin? I shared wombtime with someone else, which might explain my love of open spaces, and my tendency to live in cramped ones (more on this trend later). Unlike many other people I have no problem spending hours on end—even days in succession—by myself. Sometimes I think I can remember what it was like to be in utero, locked inside my mother's swampy trunk, nothing to do but listen to the outside world, grow, and wait for birth, my brother there beside me like a shadow, an explanation for the darkness that would so soon come to light; I reached for life and swam, elbowed my way past him to the delivery room, only to be confused by what I found there. Why so many faces? Who turned on the bright lights? My first cry must have given voice to more than shock, or fear, or a newborn's mad confusion; perhaps to careful ears there was also a hint of sadness over what I'd left behind, and a contradictory delight; after all, I had abandoned the comforts of our sleepy home, the prodigal son, born into all the love and expectations of real life.

And then I met my counterpart, my mirror image,

my five-pound-eight-ounce secret sharer. In my imagination our first moments of consciousness loom large:
both swaddled now, we rest in our mother's arms, and
I stare at this pretender to my title. He blinks his eyes
and wriggles uncomfortably. He is small, and the
nurses have left some froth above one eyebrow. His
coloring is strange, like a bruise about to blossom; in a
moment they will snatch him away from me, and
more than my beaming, exhausted mother, or the un-
masked obstetrician, or the wide-eyed attending
nurses, I will remember his face, so bewildered by the
predicament of life, so *ungrateful.* I want to console
him, when language is still just a capacity deep within
me; I want to touch him, even though sensation is
unfamiliar; then he is gone for observation, and I am
lifted from my mother's arms to discover, for the first
time, how solitude is really filled with other people,
and I am unoriginal, a copy made from disparate parts:
some drunk idea my father had, a soft place inside my
mother's arguments for equal rights, organs and fluids,
fireflies and stars. Later, in the nursery, I like to think
that I waited for Clive, and when they finally lowered
him beside me in the bassinet my unhinged gaze, for a
moment, met its weaker double, and in the course of
my hand's instinctive trip from self to other, I flashed
him an older brother's first thumbs-up sign.

After such a brilliant start, however, I was bound to
falter. Sucking, a vital instinct in every newborn, was a

problem for me. Back home now, Clive and I were each assigned a breast, mine the left, which hung a little lower with its burden, and his the right. Clive sucked happily, I am told, while I would gum my nipple, spit it out, try again without success, turn an angry color red, and howl. My parents called friends and pediatricians, met with a midwife, and consulted Dr. Spock repeatedly. They tried everything prescribed and still, feeding time was torture: I gummed and fussed until my father intervened with formula, draped in towels to protect him from the overspill. Meanwhile, Clive would smack his shiny lips, already finished with his rightful breast, and reach for mine. Soon Clive's appetite had flushed his cheeks, brightened his eyes, and started him on his way to a snowsuit of baby fat. Once I had finished dribbling formula all over my father, I would vomit. I grew skinny and turned yellow, a coloring that remained throughout my early infancy, even after I had found my appetite.

Clive's first smile was recorded during this period, a goofy, full-faced grin that followed a particularly hearty feeding. He had mastered gurgling and blowing little bubbles. My only talents, it seemed, were filling my diapers with a toxic paste indifferent to laundry detergent, and screaming at the top of my lungs.

Sadly, inexplicably, I continued to lag behind my twin brother. At three weeks he had learned to suck his thumb when he wanted to be fed, while my hands were still a mystery to me, unpredictable and vaguely threatening, like birds. I sucked my favorite pillow instead, a taste that led to a series of major suffocation scares, until my parents took my only dripping comfort away from me. At four weeks Clive's eyes stopped rolling around on their own, and focused all their helpless charm on our mother, who melted, as anyone with a heart would; when my eyes kicked in a month later, I looked right through my mother to the fuzzy blackness behind her and, later, when my eyes improved, at the large, immovable objects in our nursery: a heavy dresser filled with baby clothes and blankets; a looming wardrobe; an antique dry sink, which my parents used as a changing table and diaper-storage cabinet. The furniture frightened me. So did the telephone, which sent me into spasms when it rang, and so did our dog, Castro, a dopey yellow Labrador who was forever sniffing around my crib, sticking his nose between the wooden bars and panting at me. The same behavior made Clive's face light up. He started babbling to the dog, right on schedule, and soon he was running off at the mouth whenever he felt like it. His crib was right beside my own, and I would listen to his sweet, high voice in the stillness of our nursery. We communicated in a kind of ur-language: Clive played scales of consonants and vowels, like a musician; I answered him with long and drawn-out monosyllables. In all likelihood Clive taught me how to speak.

It was summer, our first season in the world, and a soft wind rustled the ancient maple tree outside our open windows. Cars passed by our house. So did graduate students on foot. Our parents stopped in our doorway one afternoon and listened to their children play. They were newly skeptical of many things—religion, television, government—but Clive's voice had a way of realigning their beliefs, lifting their spirits out of irony and bitterness, as if his existence, alone, were evidence of all the better things in life that might be possible, if they kept their vigilance. The dog came loping up the stairs to listen too. "Castro . . ." my father warned.

"What do you think he's saying?" my mother asked.

" 'Come clean about Vietnam,' " he said. " 'I didn't vote for President Johnson.' "

"I think," my mother answered, "he's talking to William." They listened. "See that?"

"God, that's a horrible sound."

"Give William time," my mother said. "He's just learning, that's all."

"They both can't be remarkable, right? Think of Kennedy and Johnson."

"Poor Jack."

"I know," my father said, and they shared a moment of silence.

"Still, I don't like that comparison," my mother argued.

"All right," my father said, "then he's Bobby. Or maybe Teddy, that handsome devil. They say he might turn out the best of all Joe's sons."

I don't know how long my parents stayed there. I don't know, really, if this conversation happened as I have written it. I know my parents well because they raised me, I know my brother because he is my opposite, I know the period and place because I lived in them completely. My parents are, if anything, candid in their recollections, and despite my other faults, I have a very good memory. You'll have to take my word for what you read here, though, and even if this story is more fiction than documentary evidence, it is closer to the truth of my childhood, perhaps, than mere reality. Narrativity scholars, footnote compilers, windbag experimentalists, listen up: I am one step ahead of you.

We came home from the hospital in a Volkswagen squareback to a rambling Victorian on Francis Street in Cambridge, Massachusetts. The car would later burst into flames on Route 128, and my parents, spooked by our narrow escape, would replace it with a succession of Japanese imports: a brown Toyota station wagon; matching Subarus, one with transmission trouble, the other a trick clutch; two faithful, if unexciting, Honda Civics. Our neighborhood was nothing like suburbia. The houses were big and close together, yes, and the picket fences, in the summertime, were blanketed with ivy, but the lawns remained untended when I was young, and the sidewalks carried people through our midst, not just students either: tourists on walking tours, campus security, city wanderers who had left Harvard Square to burn incense underneath the trees, stretch out on the benches, doze in the doorways of the enlightened Divinity School at the end of the street. Our house would change over time, along with the fashions of the neighborhood. As the optimism of the Great Society gave way to benign neglect, the shrubs grew unabated, and the paint peeled off the porch posts and clapboards; the middle seventies brought teal and pumpkin trim, candy-striped mailboxes, and op-art street numbers to our neighbors' houses; the white-wash of the nineteen eighties did away with all that, brought gardeners back and landscape architects to impose a sense of order; and when the money ran out in the early nineties, the shrubs returned to their unruly state, the cars on the curb shrank in size and sticker price, and the clapboards mildewed so that now, on my rare visits back, the street looks almost identical to the way it did when Clive and I were born. Through it all, unchanged at the end of Francis Street, the Gothic sanctuary of the Harvard Divinity School brought rev-

erent students from around the world to our little corner, passing our house in snow boots and in sandals, on
antique bicycles, arguing earnestly, struggling with the
weight of their textbooks and all the implications of
their theological discourse.

I would notice all of this when I was older. My
brother Clive grew into an intrepid child, and from an
early age he made a playground of our neighborhood,
unafraid of all the forces just outside the picket fence
around our yard. As a toddler he ran naked all over
Francis Street. The child Clive rode his bike in endless
circles, familiar to everyone. His interests deepened as
a teenager, and he would disappear for hours after
school, coming back with bloodshot eyes and a volume
of Thomas Aquinas, a swap for a mint-condition Silver
Surfer comic book. As an undergraduate at Harvard his
friends were free to come and go as they wanted from
our house, often staying overnight in my bedroom (I
went away to college in R——, New York, an upstate
city so dreary, I cannot bear to mention it by name);
when I came home on vacation I would find strange
clothing in my drawers, dope stashed underneath my
pillow, discarded papers on the bedside table ("Thun-
der Yonder: Morality in John Webster's *The White
Devil*" by J. P. Effendi, an "inspired" 93). I found issues of *Partisan Review* and *High Times*. Clive made
no distinctions among his friends: he spent time with
philosophers and football players, dullards and social-

ites. In his company they were all the best and the
brightest.

Except for me. No amount of babbling in the nursery, enthusiastic coaching at the breast while I
writhed, cried, and spit up my artificial formula, no
sweet gaze through the bars of my terrible crib, would
cure my stubborn ambivalence about life. To borrow a
phrase from an oft-quoted musician, I tripped at every
step in childhood.

At fourteen weeks Clive could already hold his head
in place and stare at me. Mine rolled gigantically to
the side. At twenty-eight weeks he was playing with
his feet, and reaching for everything in sight—we had
matching mobiles above our cribs, made of colorful
biomorphic shapes that held his attention for hours;
my twin mobile, like everything else, made me cry,
and when my parents took it down I cried even
harder, not as volubly, though, as when they hung it
up again, causing a tantrum so loud that I managed to
drive Castro, deaf in one ear, out into the yard to dig a
hole, either for his own grave or for mine.

One morning when we were six months old my
mother came into the nursery and found Clive sitting
up by himself. Winter had glazed the corners of our
bedroom windows with ice. The radiator hissed against
the cold New England wind that blew at will, it
seemed, through our leaky house. I had started to fuss
at her arrival, softly, even sweetly, moved by some-

thing unwanted in my diaper. "Clive," she exclaimed, followed by my father's name, "Anthony?" Clive basked in their attention that morning, showing off with his mobile, swatting at the colored shapes that hovered, for the first time, within his grasp. My father had come down the hall from his study—he was an acoustical engineer, and had cut his hours at the laboratory to help my mother around the house. "Hey," he said to Clive, "look at that, now." What smiles, and all around! I squalled louder, kicking the bars of my crib. Castro barked downstairs. Master of his head, my brother turned in my direction. He looked uncertain for a moment, wobbled, and then he fell. Both my parents sprang to his rescue, and in their haste to see that Clive hadn't hurt himself, while they soothed him with soft, tickling pinches and fervent whispers, they failed to notice a change in me. With my head pinned to its usual side, I had witnessed Clive falling backward inside his crib. An unfamiliar noise came out of my mouth. Castro climbed the stairs, and stuck his head in the doorway to watch. My parents heard me, too, staring from Clive's bedside. My mother shook her head. "Is that . . . ?" my father asked, but my smiling face had already answered his question. Before that day I had either fussed, brooded, cried, or slept uncomfortably. And now I was laughing.

My parents consulted Anna Freud's *Psychoanalysis for Teachers and Parents* and decided that, for the time being, Clive and I would benefit from spending more time together. We spent the rest of our infancy in adjoining cribs, an expensive Norwegian system recommended by a neighbor, Elias Crick, a financial consultant who smoked a pipe on his front porch, even in the middle of winter, and sold a series of products wholesale—Scandinavian furniture, vitamin supplements, exotic mushrooms—out of his basement. A new set of bars (attractive blond wood) separated the two of us while we slept, as if to keep our dreams from comingling; the rest of the time, under fairly strict supervision, we were allowed to "creep" around the crib together, babble and play, smile and stare at each other. Clive recognized his name already. I still had trouble recognizing our parents. Clive was the only thing, living or inanimate, that *didn't* scare me, and with a growing sense of alarm I watched him outgrow that Nordic prison. Just after our first birthday he walked, with my mother's help, across the creaking floorboards of our nursery. Heady moments ensued. My mother decided to give me an equal try, and she lifted me from my favorite position—flat on my back. I had goopy eyes that month, a dripping nose from allergies, and my cheeks were aflame with a skin condition. My first try ended in hysterics and toppled furniture, after Castro, no friend to this runt of the litter, charged me as if I were a pigeon. The episode set me back a few weeks, and banished Castro to the yard for

the rest of the summer, but soon enough I was following Clive on my hands and knees through the sunny
wilderness of our little ragged property, and the laby-
rinth of rooms inside our house, corralled by gates and
piled furniture. I drove Clive to distraction with my
misadventures, and continued to laugh with pleasure
every time he fell.

On Monday, February 11, 1967, at eight o'clock in
the morning, Clive began his first solo ascent of the
staircase to our nursery. We were about to enter into
our "terrible twos." At eight-fifteen Clive stopped for a
juice break, handed his bottle back to our mother, and
returned to his lonely quest for the summit. I was in
her arms, resting my head on her shoulder, groggy
from an allergy medicine that, years later, would disappear quietly from the market after being proven ad-
dictive to laboratory animals. As Clive's white,
diapered bottom disappeared around the final curve, I
coughed. Then I sneezed. Then I coughed and sneezed
at the same time, an original display of my own talents, I thought, like jazz improvisation. In a moment
Clive came tumbling back down to the spot where he
had taken his juice break. He blinked and looked
around, confused by where he found himself. *Like
birth*, I thought. My mother picked him up, kissing his
forehead, and the next thing I knew we were on our
way back to our adjoining cribs. The gate crashed
down between us. Solitary confinement suited me well,

but made Clive, a gregarious baby by all accounts, miserable. I didn't comfort him.

Psychoanalytic theory suggests that we, all of us, suffer from a malady for which Freud's science holds the only cure: *infantile amnesia*, a necessary blind-spot, or error of omission, that obscures our early childhood from the conscious surface of our lives. Name one of Dr. Rorschach's muddy pictures, stare at a shining pocket-watch, plumb the depths for painful memories, and they will take shape of their own volition, raw and uninformed by outside influences. The "talking cure" would have it that we are Beat poets, apes to all our needs, geysers of hot and true material. Anna Freud writes:

> It is just exactly this obscurity, clouding the first years of life, and the obstacles standing in the way of all efforts to get at a direct elucidation, that would make the psychoanalyst suspect something of importance was hidden there. In the same way a burglar would conclude from a specially elaborate safety lock on a safe which was very difficult to pick that his efforts would be well rewarded; people scarcely take so much trouble to lock up something worthless!

I agree and disagree with the younger Freud. Memories, of course, are never worthless, but retain their value only for the sole rememberer. To speak of them out loud is either argument, in service of a greater point, or testimony, which can be disputed. I have no illusions about my gifts. I am telling you a story, distributing my small cache of secrets one by one, mixing legal tender with invented currency so that everything might circulate, *e pluribus unum*. As if, after everything, God existed.

What about Oedipus, his unnatural Queen Jocasta, and the ugliness at the crossroads of Phocis? Did I, like every son (allegedly), harbor a nasty castration-complex? Unlikely business at our house on Francis Street. My parents, conscious of tradition's inequalities, fulfilled almost identical roles in the family, and as breast feeding gave way to bottles, and little jars of Gerber baby food, *mother* and *father* became interchangeable words in our vocabulary. My mother returned to part-time work. She held degrees in philosophy and computer science, and contributed to pioneering advances in computer programming. Punch cards (remember them?) were forever falling from her handbag in those early years, and lay around the house in bundled stacks, food for hungry mainframe computers, those dinosaurs of wire, tapes, and tubes that would soon be extinct. My father was the better cook, an avid gardener, the art and opera lover, while my mother's concerns were far more practical: household repairs, saving money for our college education, balancing the family checkbook. This is not to say she lacked a creative spark; on the contrary, marriage to my politically Maoist father must have made her something of a mental escape artist, just to counteract his daily speeches about grain harvests, and unemployment in the steel belt. When I was older I would learn that my mother had money of her own, nothing spectacular, just enough to take the edge off her decisions about life and work, and to explain the many contradictions of my upbringing. We struggled, but never wanted for anything. We were no better than middle Americans, just different. My mother's study on the small and seldom-used third floor of our house was the site of her independent wealth, where she explored her interests underneath the watchful eyes of our sepia-toned New England–eccentric ancestors. She learned FORTRAN at that very rolltop desk, something her great-great-aunt Madeline, woman suffragist with satin gloves and parasol, would have bragged about. Her grandfather Percy, poet laureate of Bar Harbor, might have been baffled by her selections from the Modern Library, but he would have found his full set of Edward Gibbon's *The Decline and Fall of the Roman Empire* in excellent condition. Our charmed neighborhood was filled with variations of a similar pattern: two parents, a job and a half between them, hidden capital that gave them time to spare for bright, precocious children. They were

blessed, to be sure, but their politics demanded a retreat from 1950s consumerism and its paranoid Cold
War underpinnings. When my father's oxford shirts
began to fray, and his dungarees lost their color, he
gave them to my mother, who mended them and kept
them for herself. In good weather many of our neighbors—Judith Freedlander, a leggy physician; the
historian Arnold Zimmerman; Elias Crick, already
mentioned—took their bicycles to work, complete with
baskets for their briefcases, and bells to alert preoccu-
pied students. Their idealism found a perfect home in
Cambridge, where it combined with the indifference of
inherited money, and Yankee thrift. In a way our
neighborhood was a utopian experiment, like Haw-
thorne's Brook Farm, or a cross between the Playboy
mansion (nudity, recreational drugs) and a Shaker village (pacifism, unfinished wood), and if that means my
parents' ideals were doomed to fail (remember the
eighties?), then I can live with the disappointments we
faced as a family, knowing that ideal happiness can
live only in daydreams, Hollywood movies, or between
the protective covers of a sentimental book.

For trips around the block my parents invested in a
deluxe carriage for two from the Sears catalog, not the
side-by-side, open-air model so common in this age of
infertility treatments, but a serious front-to-back, twin-
cabin sedan with spring suspension, a roll bar, a thick
blue canvas body, and a retractable canopy over each

sleeping compartment for either a sunny "open boat"
or shady "covered wagon" feel. At first I rode up front
(seniority), hidden underneath my canvas hood, a cotton baby blanket, and a hand-knit cap to protect my
scalp from the elements; Clive preferred the backseat,
top down, of course, seat belt loose around his waist so
he could lift his arms up to the sky and feel the wind
of travel through his fingers. His hair would flutter, I
am told. Yes, he babbled, and charmed neighbors and
passersby alike with his big bright eyes and easy smile.
"I'm in love," a stunning undergraduate would say,
leaning in to get a closer look; at that point she would
notice my listless bundle in the other seat, having mis-
taken me, at first glance, for groceries. "Are they . . .
twins?" she would ask uncertainly, trying to reconcile
our differences. To cut down on the tedious and potentially damaging explanations, I think, my parents sent
me to the back of the baby carriage, although in later
years, when I recalled to them my frustration at always having to take the rear—on car trips, plane rides,
even in the swan boats at Boston Common—they
claimed never to have segregated me. Some of my
most vivid childhood memories, however, involve the
distinct possibility of being left behind while Clive
charged bravely through new and puzzling environ-
ments. At the New England Aquarium I spent a terrifying quarter hour alone with the penguins, before my
mother returned with Clive pressed in her arms, run-

ning in place. Deep in the basement of the Peabody
Museum at Harvard, where we had been banished after Clive, not even two, had tried to smash open a
display case and crush a portion of their glass flower
collection, which he had found pedantic, my father left
me to die at the foot of a Kwakiutl totem pole while
he tried to locate my brother, who had gone off to
hunt the Pacific Northwest. Mostly I remember, with
the exaggerated clarity of an antihistamine buzz, the
back of my brother's head growing smaller while he
crawls, walks, and begins to run ahead of me.

When it came to toilet training Clive, again, was
unbeatable. He had grown into a little man already, a
Green Beret in diapers, capable of any test of skill he
put his mind to. My allergies prevented me from getting around much in the warmer months, while in the
winter I developed chronic eczema, a painful rash that
started at my fingertips, and in the arches of my
sweaty feet, migrating from there until the two tribes
of blisters met on my upper body, trading their discomfort like so many trinkets. Sunlight helped, but
there was little of it during those endless New England
winters. Instead my parents greased me from head to
toe with Eucerin cream, and I slipped around the
house like a landlocked Channel swimmer. During the
summer of our second year Clive, after five successful
trips to the potty in one afternoon, was pronounced

"anal expressive." Whenever Clive heard the phrase his eyes lit up, and he pulled his diaper down in recognition. I spent agonizing, fruitless hours on the same potty seat, supervised by my mother, who brought paperwork to better pass the time. I could hear my expressive brother playing in the yard with Castro and a baby-sitter. I strained, whimpered, cried out, and fell asleep. My mother sighed on the edge of the bathtub, unstrapping me from my ignoble throne. Nobody likes a dull, retentive king.

Every morning, for a while, my father, Clive, and I met in the bathroom for a "tinkle" seminar, where I proved myself to be a natural in the subtle art of urinating. Clive was reluctant to harness the energy of his waterfall, spraying an innocent, golden shower, more often than not, all over the bathroom. He tinkled on the floor, in the wicker trash can, turned, and made a lovely arc into the tub. My father pretended to get upset, but Clive's laughter was so contagious, his performance so inspired that, in the end, who could mind? Rolls of toilet paper disappeared in sacrifice. "Done," Clive would announce, and run off to his next diversion. My father, cleaning up on his hands and knees already, would shake his head and chuckle. My own work was careful, studious, and precise, and because of that it took a while. The open toilet yawned at me. Would I fall in? "Good boy," my father encouraged, but any words of praise distracted me. The stream would stop, and I would start to blubber. Frustration was my constant companion during all my early years.

Clive's first word had been the charming and unlikely *Castro,* spoken while he tried to ride the dog across the living room. Mine was *Ouch,* whined in the pediatrician's office during an outpatient procedure to remove an infected splinter from my heel. Clive followed his first word up with complicated phrases, sounding vaguely British, like *Mum and Da; Lovey dovey, of course;* and *Goodness, naptime?* Language, to me, revolved around discomfort and bodily injury, as in *I hurt,* or *Ouch, my finger.*

But even then, early in our lives together, Clive was sympathetic to my trouble, and when he wasn't running wild through the yard, hanging all over Castro, or moving furniture, he kept a quiet vigil at my bedside. If I was up and diapered, he brought me blocks, one by one, and helped me stack them into towers, which he couldn't resist knocking over, teaching me a valuable lesson about the vicissitudes of life, and human nature. Clive taught me how to transform walking into running, a wild state of freedom that addicted me, I think, to growing up. All my early trouble seemed to disappear on summer evenings in our yard, the upstairs windows filled with light, neighbors on the back porch drinking cocktails and talking politics, passing a joint between them; the dog barked at nothing in particular and Clive, shedding his clothes and diapers, ran circles while I tried to follow him, my image in a better mirror, my perfect little self. We were still unaware, in any real way, of the adult world and all its compromises, we were simply running until our legs fell out from underneath us, pitching through the dark until we hit the ground with a double thump. My mother stood up from her Adirondack chair. Someone had just said, "Eugene McCarthy." Clive giggled. I blew my nose, and she sat down again. My father coughed and handed her the last of their communal weed.

And when our faces swelled with the need for sleep, and even Clive began to sniffle, my mother left her sixties politics behind and brought us up to bed—Clive just took her hand and walked himself, while I melted into her arms and let the liquor on her breath clear out my sinuses. She was used to the way I leaked fluid on her clothing, and didn't seem to mind. "Bedtime?" Clive asked on our way up the staircase.

"Yes," my mother answered, "it's bedtime."

"Buh," I tried, hoping for similar praise.

"Bedtime," she corrected me. "But that's a good try, William."

"Bedtime," Clive repeated to himself. "Bedtime, bedtime, bedtime."

"Buh," I tried again.

"Almost," my mother said, but it was too late for encouragement. I had already started crying.

Later that night, after a dual cleanup, a change into our loose summer pajamas, and a hurried storytime, and after our mother, satisfied that we had drifted off somewhere sweetly unconscious, had slipped back to her cocktail party, Clive rustled in his sheets until he woke me. I could hear him breathing in the adjoining crib, but I couldn't see him in the dark. "Buh," he said, for no other reason than to comfort me.

"Buh," I answered sleepily. I was too exhausted to hate him for his kindness, and grateful, to be honest, that he should be so near.

"Buh."

"Buh."

In other words, Good night.

A year passed between summers, and the mismatched twins turned three on a rainy day in June. Our house filled with other parents and their children, some of whom we'd never met. Clive's hair had grown into a shining Beatles-style mop, not studied, like Paul Mc-Cartney's, but more playful, like Ringo Starr's in *A Hard Day's Night.* My mother, no artist with the scissors, had run into some trouble with a cowlick on my

top, and I looked more like a lesbian, or David Bowie
in his glitter years. My brother spent the afternoon
enchanting the aloof Faith Crick—even at the age of
three a stunning beauty—with Castro as a willing
partner, licking or wagging on command, rushing any
toddler who attempted cutting in. As always, I attracted the strange, serious girl with poor social skills;
this time it was Dorothea Zimmerman, twice my size
and three years older. Clive and Faith sat on the floor
playing earnestly, while Dorothea followed me from
room to room, trying to hand me things: Castro's soggy
tennis ball, a throw pillow, an orphaned suede mocca-
sin with fringe. Cake time distracted Dorothea, but
only as long as it took to eat her slice without a fork,
and then she started in again, lumbering behind me to
the delight of all the parents, who felt sorry for poor
Dorothea already, and thought we'd make a cute—if
asymmetrical—couple. We had a "groovy" soundtrack
to our chase scene, Ravi Shankar, and I stumbled over
each lumpy throw pillow in my path only to encounter
another one. She cornered me by the terrarium, where
my parents were trying to grow three different kinds
of moss. A sloppy chocolate kiss from her reduced me
to hysterics, and brought an end to my afternoon of
socializing. I still remember being snatched up in my
father's arms and carried through the party on my way
upstairs to exile. Lovely, complicated Faith looked up

from her action painting, turned to Clive, and whispered something in his ear. He ignored her, and continued his automatic-writing project.

Later that same year we were tested by a developmental psychologist in preparation for day care and, soon afterward, kindergarten. They ushered us into separate cubicles and asked us, with a bribe of apple juice, to perform simple tasks with blocks, play word games with a graduate student, and answer hypothetical questions to the best of our knowledge. Our father sat nearby, in case of a tantrum, reading *Scientific American.* Clive and I both recognized, I think, the seriousness of the task, and we concentrated hard. While our little minds were picked, pushed, and prodded, our father flipped through his magazine, yawning. Afterward he treated us to ice cream at Swensen's in Harvard Square, a gloomy parlor, usually empty, which served its desserts in dirty aluminum cups. We shared a sundae quietly until Clive claimed the maraschino cherry for himself, and in the ensuing fight my father promised never again to serve us sugar on an empty stomach.

The day the tests came back, later in the fall, was one of the happiest in my entire childhood. As expected, Clive's scores were excellent, placing him among the highest-percentile groups in every category. He took the news well, blushing modestly when my mother kissed his forehead, running off to find a

prized stick that he had lent to Castro, generously, earlier in the day. My performance came as a complete
surprise. Somehow, despite the differences between us
in size, skill level, and temperament, my test scores
were either identical to Clive's, or higher.

My parents *flipped*, in a word. My mother spent an
hour on the phone, calling friends, relatives, and in-
laws, stared at me lovingly, searched through unfamiliar cookbooks for a cake recipe. When my father came
home from work, he called me in for a rare visit to his
study, where he put me on his knee and showed me
pages of his careful calculations on graph paper, organized neatly in a spiral binder. Sunlight streamed
through the windows. Dust from a nearby bookshelf
and his ashtray, filled with blackened pipe tobacco and
the fruitless ends of many joints, in combination,
rocked my body with a fit of sneezing. When it was
over, my father wiped his page dry with a napkin, and
closed the binder. "Another time," he said. "Let's see
what your brother's doing."

We descended the stairs together, his big creak followed by my little one, and found my brother in the
kitchen, helping my mother with the cake, which
would end up charred, but no matter: an independent,
unbiased panel of judges had found me equal to, if not
better than, my remarkable twin.

Identical twins are an anomaly of nature whereby a
fertilized ovum, or "the miracle of life," divides in two,

resulting in genetically identical zygotes, which pro-
ceed to find themselves a soft cradle in the wall of the
uterus; they grow together in their sleep until the cradle tips them out, first one, and then the other, and
they tumble into consciousness, and competition for
the most coveted prize of childhood: parental love. Is
this where the similarity between them ends, or is it
only just beginning? What about the clinical studies
that would prove, beyond the shadow of any skeptic's
doubt, that monozygotic twins (identical, in other
words) follow paths that are, in effect, preordained,
subject to the selfsame tastes, whims, talents? *Bunk*, I
say to the new determinism. And what's my scientific
proof? Keep reading. . . .

Instead of regular nursery school we attended a
children's *Hort*, based on the Viennese model, the
brainchild of local parents who were convinced that
traditional schooling methods would neglect the needs
of their unusually bright children. The *Hort* met every
afternoon in the basement of a Unitarian church on
Wendell Street, on the other side of the Divinity
School from our neighborhood. The space was also
rented out to therapy groups, and donated to political
action committees—a bulletin board in the corner advertised protests and meetings, and was decorated with
a portrait of the late Reverend Martin Luther King,
Jr., white doves and peace signs, and the single, raised
fist of the Black Power movement. We had no

chalkboards in the *Hort*, no workbooks, and no curriculum. If we needed toys to pass the time, we manufactured them as a group. Army cots—but no pillows—
were provided at naptime, and stuffed animals, favorite blankets, or any other "transitional objects" were
forbidden. We had a different *Verwalter* every week,
who led us through exercises designed to build our
self-esteem, encourage our creativity, and enhance our
practical skills. Like assembly workers we built identical puppet theaters out of cardboard boxes, painted Expressionist self-portraits, and made kinetic sculptures
out of coat hangers, yarn, and empty aluminum trays
from Swanson TV dinners, the "detritus," we were lectured, "of a postindustrial society." Once a month our
parents came to meet with a *Verwalter* about our progress while we played nearby in a wooden pen. Their
voices, scarcely more than whispers, echoed in the
empty classroom. "Clive," it was reported, "is thriving
at the *Hort.* His transition from work to play is effortless. The other children just adore him, and he obviously takes pleasure in their company. As a matter of
fact, they seem to have elected him some kind of
leader in a natural democratic process, and look to him
for guidance in times of trouble. Have you seen his
puppet theater? It's *brilliant.*"

When discussion turned to me, the *Verwalter* put on
a pair of half-glasses and consulted her notes. "William's time here, as of yet, has been undistinguished.

He ignores the other children, and they in turn pay no
mind to him. He never completed his puppet theater,
tore up his self-portrait before it was finished, and his
mobile—how shall I put it?—was a *less than average*
construction. There are times, of course, when he
shows great potential. Just last week he told one of my
colleagues about a dream in vivid detail, something
about snakes and witches, which sounded fascinating.
When he does speak his vocabulary is quite ad-
vanced—if unusual—but mostly, I'm afraid, William
is uncommunicative. Perhaps with a brother of Clive's
caliber, William is undergoing an identity crisis. We
fear for the quality of his future. . . ."

And so the first grave sentence had been passed
against me, branding my forehead, and my educational
record, with a U, for *underachiever*. I didn't know it
then, but this label would haunt me throughout my
childhood, and adolescence, and well into my adult
life, which I will get to eventually. Like a middle-class
Hester Prynne progressive society had deemed me
guilty of something unforgivable, and saw to it that I
would suffer for squandering my talent, privilege, and
early access to such enlightened ideals—all the gifts
that set them apart from the mainstream of society, or
so my parents believed. I may be overstating my case,
but the point remains: that hovering, invisible U became my ally, my conscience, a dear and loyal friend
when I most needed one. Who else would see me

through the endless turmoil of growing up? What could ease my anxiety? My parents were idealists and professionals, busy with the work of their generation, building what they thought would be a Great Society. Clive tried his best, at different times, to help me on his golden path, and regardless of whether he did it out of brotherly love, or an inherited interest in community service, he lacked a willing victim. I am proud to be a disappointment to almost everybody. Lend me money, and I will never pay you back. Fall in love with me, and I will fail to acknowledge you. Save your compassion for someone who really needs it, I am well engaged, trying to be my own worst enemy. I would call this my manifesto, or autobiography, but that would mean I have an ideal audience in mind.

Call it a diary.

II. Latency and Adolescence

The remainder of my childhood consisted of a series of freak injuries, stealthy illnesses, and periods of bed rest to recuperate. I didn't *grow up* so much as I *got better*. When I was four, mumps stole an entire summer, and my birthday party that year—a hushed, family-only affair in my sickroom—felt somehow funereal. I remember the cake appearing suddenly in my delirium, and the way the birthday candles eluded my hot, mentholated breath. Clive made his birthday wish for me,

a sweet, sentimental "I hope William gets better" wor-
thy of Charles Dickens. I kept my dark wish to myself:
that Clive might get sick instead.

Five brought stitches, a frostbitten finger, measles,
and a head-lice infestation, in that order. We attended
kindergarten in the morning that year, and in the afternoon we returned to the children's *Hort* for observation. It was in a sandbox on the church grounds
that, following the head-lice epidemic, I lifted a full
plastic bucket too quickly and threw out my back for a
week. At six I suffered from chicken pox, a reflower-
ing of my eczema, and a badly sprained ankle. Seven
proved to be a quiet year: more head lice, allergies in
the spring, and a minor concussion (dodgeball accident), but otherwise I felt stronger than ever. I had
finally caught up on my schoolwork after so many
absences, and my homeroom teacher at the Agassiz
School had made some encouraging remarks about a
report I had written on Tenzing Norgay, the Sherpa
who climbed Mount Everest with Edmund Hillary.
My father read the paper over and pronounced it
"well organized" and "insightful." It ended up on the
refrigerator, right next to Clive's comparison of com-
edy and tragedy in the works of Shakespeare and the
Three Stooges, which prefigured the high/low obsession of many contemporary scholars. In gym class I
had finished, for the first time, the twelve-minute run,
and received an honorary orange ribbon; team cap-

tains no longer picked me just to make my brother, the perennial superstar, happy; during a gymnastics exhibition I experienced my first taste of love and lust in combination when Faith Crick, already willowy, performed a split on the balance beam in a baggy leotard, oblivious to the consequences. I saw God in her error, and blushed for Him. Clive, I think, was never the same, and pursued her relentlessly until we were eleven, when she finally agreed to wear his "Students for Stevenson" button to school, a gift from my father, and already a collector's item. They were a couple through all our years in Cambridge, and I was—not so secretly either—in love with my brother's girlfriend. But all that would come later.

At eight I contracted strep throat and mononucleosis simultaneously, bringing my recent progress to an untimely end. In the middle of February I took to my bed again, and I would stay there under quarantine for the rest of the school year. I remember a glass thermometer, cold towels on my forehead, and a bowl of chipped ice beside my bed. My parents lowered themselves to buying Jell-O only after the doctor had recommended it, and rolled their black-and-white, seldom-used television into my bedroom as a last resort against ennui. A strange gray glow kept me company all day while I half slept, and when school was over Clive would bring Castro in to see me, and the three of us watched reruns together: *Leave It to Beaver, Father*

Knows Best, A Family Affair, shows our parents hated
with an equal venom. Clive became convinced that
Mr. French was an escaped convict, and watched each
episode of *A Family Affair* carefully for clues about his
past. He found a pattern in the shade of his turtle-
necks, but nothing more substantial. Already he could
tell a sign from the signified, like a little Deconstruc-
tionist—in New Haven, just down Route 95, Paul de
Man had introduced the academy to Jacques Derrida
in *Blindness and Insight* (1971), but few, beyond Clive,
were listening. I was too weak to follow his investiga-
tions, but Clive would talk to me anyway. "His beard,"
Clive insisted, "means something. Do you think he was
a pirate?" I was propped up on three pillows, weak-
ened, in pain.

"Lozenge," I managed.

Clive opened a tin of Sucrets and unwrapped one
for me. "Secret agent, then."

I swallowed the lozenge by mistake, and started
coughing. Castro limped away (arthritis).

"Mom," Clive cried, "William's coughing."

My mother came upstairs shortly with ice cream for
both of us, and a fresh towel for my forehead. Clive
was back on the floor again, legs crossed, studying the
television intently.

"That's right," he told Mr. French, "give her a lecture. That Buffy's a pain in the ass."

"Language," my mother reminded him.

Clive ate his ice cream happily. When he was finished, and my mother had left us alone to return to her own study, Clive licked his spoon and watched me. The bowl of ice cream rested in my lap untouched. I shivered from the change in temperature. "Are you done with that?" he asked.

"No," I answered weakly.

By April I could leave my bed again, and take short walks around the house. My father had bought me a flannel bathrobe at the Harvard Coop, cotton pajamas, and a pair of sheepskin slippers at least two sizes too big, while my mother had arranged for Clive to bring special homework assignments back and forth from school. They set a rocking chair by my bedroom window, and I spent most of my time there in the rain-soaked sunlight, a workbook open in my lap, looking out at Francis Street through the limbs of the giant maple tree in our front yard. I watched squirrels cross power lines and jump down to a lower perch and freeze, while neighborhood cats stalked bugs and birds through the grass, taking off when a group of students passed in mismatched hats and slickers, trailing smoke, and sophisticated laughter.

Every day I watched Clive come home from the end of the street, usually with friends, and he would bring them in the yard to stand below my window for company. In my memory it is always raining; after all, springtime is monsoon season in New England. "Hey,

William!" he yelled up to me, hair wet, poncho dripping. Clive's friends would have done anything for
him, up to and including standing in the rain to cheer
up his sickly brother. They were the first of his apos-
tles, and I knew they didn't like me. I waved from
behind the glass, sipping hot lemonade sweetened with
raw honey. "Hey, William," they repeated. I suppose
they were waiting for me to open the window and say
something, but I was under doctor's orders to avoid the
open air. Slowly, they dispersed. "Bye, William," I
heard, snicker included, something Clive, the eternal
optimist, would never have suspected from his friends.
I heard him come inside, take off his rubber boots in
the front hallway, and walk softly in his stocking feet
upstairs. "Castro," he called. The aging dog groaned to
attention somewhere in the house, and followed him.
Would the rain clouds ever leave our end of Francis
Street? Would I ever feel better?

"Tube time," Clive announced, tossing my homework on the foot of my bed and settling into my bright
red beanbag chair, an early birthday present to lift my
sagging spirits. "C-minus again."

"I don't care."

"You should."

"What's on TV?" I asked.

"Cold War propaganda," he said in my father's
words. "You want a Popsicle or something?"

A heat wave hit the Northeast coast at the end of

June that year, and took up residence with the help of an unfriendly tropical current named El Niño. Luckily I was no longer bedridden, and passed those shirtless, barefoot days in the shade of the back porch, sipping herbal iced tea with Clive while we assembled puzzles on a plywood table, or filled up books of easy crosswords. Our mother sunbathed topless in the backyard, lying on a ratty towel. Our father preferred full-frontal nudity, and would emerge from the house already in the buff after a morning of work, squinting in the doorway for a moment before he crossed the lawn, and took his place beside my mother. All the neighbors were doing it: the Zimmermans next door were famous for their nude gardening, and Dorothea, sadly, had inherited their green thumb, and often waved to me while she tended her radish patch. The adult bodies I had seen looked suspiciously soft, way too white, and unbelievably hairy, like nothing that should be exposed to sunlight.

"Dad," Clive would ask, fitting a puzzle piece into place, "what's so great about nudity?" I kept my eyes on the puzzle, a Dutch landscape of tulips surrounding a quaint antique windmill. The box claimed it was of moderate difficulty, but I had no idea where to begin.

"It's natural," my father answered, stretching out on his towel, "and beautiful. Some people don't like the human body, but they're usually Republicans."

Clive already felt an allegiance to the Democratic

party, and slipped his shorts down to the floor. Refreshed, he found a crucial piece of the puzzle, and fit it into place. I felt a little queasy, and reported this fact to my mother.

"Maybe," she said, unpeeling an orange, "you should take your shorts off like Clive. You'd be cooler that way."

"I'm *very* cool," Clive announced.

My father knelt beside my mother and began spreading body oil on her shoulders. His "penis" (they were fond of clinical terms) swelled and stirred. Clive fitted into place a bright red tulip blossom and I had seen enough, taking my shame inside where I could live with it, and try to forget what I had just seen in my own backyard. A poster of Hieronymus Bosch's medieval masterpiece *The Garden of Earthly Delights* hung in the living room during those years, as if in explanation, and I used to stare at this picture for hours, certain that I would find among the scenes of violence and drunken revelry an example from my life on Francis Street.

The three of them were incorrigible nudists, and I learned to dread trips to the beach, which began with a sweltering car ride to the North Shore, foul-mouthed Castro panting and drooling in my ear, progressed into a "long march" through the burning sand to a rocky, isolated spot where like-minded perverts openly convened. My family disrobed, cleared the cigarette butts,

Popsicle sticks, and other debris from the gravel, and spread a communal blanket out on the uneven ground. Our nearest neighbors, another nudist family, would smile in our direction. Middle-aged men wore sunglasses to disguise their gawking. Every now and then a few stray boys would wander over from the "square" beach, push each other, giggle, shout "Titties," and take off running. The nudists turned the other cheek. Now I ask you, could Hieronymus himself have painted such a picture of the end of civilization, complete with garbage in the sand, painful sunburn, and Indian tapestries? I huddled in my towel and looked at the horizon, trying to will a storm of some kind that would end my humiliation-by-the-sea.

On the car ride back Clive would ask, "Mom, how come William won't take his clothes off in public?"

"Ask your brother," my father suggested from the driver's seat.

Clive asked me.

"Just because," I told Clive.

His skin, that summer, turned a deep, golden brown. Mine peeled off in sheets, like wax paper. My nose and the rest of my face were different colors entirely.

"What William means," my mother said, "is that he's sublimated his natural urge to be more grown-up. He's in the middle of what psychoanalysts call a *latency period*."

Clive thought about it. "I'm not latent, am I?"

"Sure you are," my father said, adjusting his straw hat. "Just not to the same degree. Latency is a natural stage, Clive, and William should be open to it."

"You're latent," Clive told me.

"Shut up," I said.

"William," my mother warned.

"How about," my father suggested, trying to pre-empt an argument, "we go to Woodman's for some onion rings."

It should come as no surprise, then, given the pre-vailing vocabulary, that Clive and I would find our-selves, before the age of twelve, undergoing biweekly psychoanalytic treatments with Dr. Sibyl Strauss, who specialized in tormenting the children of Boston's in-tellectual class. We had grown too old for the chil-dren's *Hort,* and our parents knew that puberty was fast approaching, when our hormones would awaken a napping libido, and high school would take us on its magic carpet ride to young adulthood. They sought, in the words of Anna Freud, to "establish from the out-side a reasonable agreement between the child's ego, the urge of his impulses, and the demands of society."

Every other Wednesday afternoon our mother picked us up in front of the Agassiz School and drove us to Newton, the suburb of choice for progressive Bos-tonians, and dropped us off at Sibyl's office, in the ground floor of her town house. To be fair, Sibyl's practice, at that time, was widely admired, and she adhered to strict and responsible professional standards, unlike many other torturers of her kind, judging by the content of talk shows I've seen on the subject. She served us ginger ale in her waiting room, spiked creatively with raisins, which sank to the bottom of her plastic tumblers and rose again to the surface, as if for air, carried by carbonated bubbles. This wartime amusement seemed charming in the dawning age of Pong and Space Invaders.

Sibyl kept her office closed off from the rest of her house with sliding wooden doors, which shut behind us with a definitive *thunk*. She had decorated the waiting room with a diverse collection of African masks, early American furniture, and etchings by the Swiss artist Paul Klee, two of which I remember: *The Hero with the Wing*, a deformed ex-warrior with his one human arm in a sling, the stump of a wing with shorn feathers in place of the other; the equally disturbing *Virgin in a Tree*, a reclining nude whose limbs, it seemed, were made of the same gnarled wood as the skeletal tree branches that supported her. Our natural defenses, then, were softened by the novelty of Sibyl's ginger ale, and the spectacle of Modernism.

I always sat with Sibyl first in her little office, scarcely bigger than her mahogany desk and the leather couch I napped on. She kept a window cracked for ventilation—Sibyl chain-smoked brown Nat Shermans—but otherwise the room was dark and unnaturally humid, and the walls seemed vaguely to be alive, probably an intentional simulation of the womb. The only light came from a banker's lamp on Sibyl's desk, which allowed her to take notes on a yellow legal pad. Her Hannah Arendt bun made her look sixty, but Sibyl had just turned forty-three the year we saw her—I learned her age much later, when her divorce from a philandering cardiologist received full coverage in *The Boston Globe*. My sensitive eyes watered in her gloomy cloud of secondhand cigarette smoke. She asked the usual questions in a detached, clinical manner: memories of early childhood, recurring dreams or fantasies, nocturnal emissions (yes or no), masturbatory habits (objects of desire, how frequently). After a few visits I could see that my fears, as crippling as I found them, were too mundane for her: run-of-the-mill abandonment, familiar darkness, boring strangers in the closet. While her cigarette burned in a humming, ineffective smokeless ashtray, she tried out other, more tantalizing possibilities. "Do you ever dream," she asked, "about your mother?"

"Sure," I answered, through allergic tears.

"Good." She marked something in her notes. "And have these dreams ever been accompanied by [pause while she takes a drag] an *erection?*"

"No, Dr. Strauss."

"Sibyl," she corrected me.

"No, Sibyl."

"Very well, then. And your father," she pronounced, switching gears, "how do you feel about him?" She lit a new cigarette with the burning end of her last, eyeing me.

"I love him, I guess."

"You love him," she said, sounding disappointed. She marked her notes again, repeating out loud, *"He loves him, he guesses."* In my company her dreams of ground-breaking papers and international conferences conducted in the German language all evaporated. She shuffled the papers on her desk and took notes silently until our hour together was up. "You can go now," she told me without lifting her eyes. "Tell Clive I'm ready to see him." In the waiting room Clive dropped his *Architectural Digest,* nodded silently, and took my place in Sibyl's office. I would spend the next hour trying to figure out what I had done wrong, under the watchful eyes of those almond masks, Freud's *uncanny* come to wooden life. Clive and Sibyl's voices murmured softly behind the door. The knotty virgin taunted me. I finished my ginger ale, flat now, and chewed my raisins. When Clive's hour was up, he emerged from the office wiping his eyes with a handkerchief that Sibyl had given him, the concerned psychoanalyst in tow.

"Remember," she told Clive, "have your mother fill a hot water bottle before bed, and keep it underneath your pillow."

He thanked her, wiping his nose.

"Wait beside William until your mother comes." Sibyl disappeared into her office.

"What happened?" I asked Clive, but he would never tell me.

"Privileged information," he claimed, pulling a stack of baseball cards out from his back pocket. Whatever childhood trauma Clive had just unearthed, he recovered instantly. "Who would you rather have batting cleanup, Jim Rice or Freddy Lynn?"

Clive and I had been sleeping in separate bedrooms for a few years now, a split precipitated by the kind of crackpot book on childhood development my parents were forever discovering, trumpeting for a while, and then denouncing to anyone who would listen. The truth is, after my annual periods of quarantine, I was happy to be alone. Clive had taken the room beside my father's study, and filled it with his records, books, and comics, all filed and cataloged neatly. Every morning, before Clive came downstairs for breakfast, he made his bed, and every afternoon he checked his various collections for gaps and alphabetical mistakes, cleaned his records, dusted his books and comics. Once a week he vacuumed his entire room. A single poster hung on his wall, framed in plastic, Carlton "Pudge"

Fisk hitting his miracle home run over the Green Monster to win game six of the 1975 World Series. His view from the window included the ancient maple tree, a corner of our front yard, a stretch of sidewalk, and a healthy piece of Francis Street, an ordinary neighborhood tableau; at night, however, Clive's window had secret visual access to the Cricks' house across the street, and more important, Faith Crick's holy bedroom, which revealed itself at certain hours for his private audience, or so he told me after they had broken up for good in college.

I stayed in our first room, the former nursery, which I converted, all on my own, into a trash bin and laundry hamper. I tossed my comics, when I had finished reading them, underneath my bed. Records roasted on every windowsill. My Red Sox poster—Rick "The Rooster" Burleson, contact-hitting shortstop—was perpetually falling on the foot of my bed. I will spare you the more gruesome details, just to say that, anally speaking, we had pulled a switcheroo.

At night I lay in bed and listened to my garbage settle, and to our house, which literally groaned, ticked like a bomb, and made other *undead* noises that frightened me into insomnia. Did I miss the familiar presence of my twin? Possibly. Outside, I could hear my mother bringing Clive his nightly prescription, the red hot water bottle, to ease his difficult passage into sleep. "Thanks, Mom," he said. She kissed his forehead. On her way back down the hallway she would stop at my bedroom door, fight against the accumulated trash to force it open, and peek inside.

"If you don't clean this," she reminded me, "no one else will."

"I know that, Mom."

"Sleep well," she said, pulling the door shut. I really was afraid of the dark, and climbed out of bed for a piece of the hallway's light, stepping from sweatshirt, to damp towel, to open textbook, like rocks in a foul stream. Once I had opened the door a crack, I could go back to bed, and try to ignore the nighttime racket. Castro, about to die of a tumor, yawned and shook his tags at the foot of the stairs. My parents murmured to each other in the kitchen. I heard Rick Burleson double over at shortstop, threatening to fall. Clive started snoring, and I tried my best to follow him.

After we had been visiting Dr. Strauss in Newton for a few months, our parents called a family meeting to discuss our progress over a casserole dinner. They wanted everything to be out in the open, they said, so that each of us might better understand the psychoanalytic process, a sometimes confusing "ego experience," as they put it.

Let me describe the scene: Clive sits at the head of the table, I sit at the foot, with our parents on the same side between us. We have just finished a heated discussion about a dark-horse presidential candidate named Jimmy Carter. Fleetwood Mac plays on the stereo, loud enough to annoy, too quiet—thankfully— to really hear. Castro sleeps nearby, uninterested in the organic experimental food we are forced to eat. My father wears a red-and-white-checked gingham shirt and blue jeans. My mother wears a hand-embroidered denim shirt, and a skirt she has made out of a tapestry and wornout dungarees from my father's early-seventies collection. Clive looks sharp in his striped T-shirt and Toughskins. I have overdone it again, coupling my own Toughskins with a matching jacket, a full, horrible suit. Taken together, our hair could stuff a sofa, easily.

"What you both need to know," my mother tells us, "is that you're healthy, well-adjusted boys. I mean, we knew this already, but now we know it deeply."

"That's right," my father says, "two sensitive, caring, democratic individuals." He sips wine from a coffee mug. "We're proud of you."

Clive has just recently regressed from a hot water bottle to an old stuffed animal named Other Bear, a move my parents, and Dr. Strauss, consider progress. I have finally cleaned my room but, in the process, threw out most of my belongings in a fit of pique, including my poster of "The Rooster," which saddens me.

"Clive has been working out some issues in his dream life," my mother continues, "which can be a frightening thing." Clive eats steadily, as if she is talking about someone else. "At times like this it's not uncommon to regress a little, and lower the proportion of instinct restriction."

"Isn't that right, Clive?" my father asks.

Clive lifts his plate off the table and licks it clean. "Right."

"Now, William," my mother says, "there's something we need to discuss with you. But I have to warn you first, you might find it embarrassing."

I stare at the ruin of my plate, dreading the conversation. "Can I please be excused?"

"Not yet," my father chimes in. He watches me carefully, his strictest form of discipline. "You listen, too, Clive."

My mother leans in my direction. "I hope you know that masturbation isn't dirty, or wrong, or unnatural. It's *good*, William. You shouldn't be afraid of your sexuality, or anything else that makes you feel good. In moderation, of course."

"As long as you're safe and responsible," my father adds. "From what I understand, Clive is a regular masturbator, and I'm sure he could give you some tips."

"Can I be excused?" I ask again.

"Not until we're done talking," my mother tells me. "Please?"

Clive watches me wither in the spotlight. "Let him go, already."

My parents look at each other, frowning. In situations like this our family operates under a democratic system where each family member casts an equal vote. In the event of a tie Castro sides with me and Clive—a hard-won idea of my brother's, which has proven itself to be a stroke of constitutional brilliance. They can see that we have beaten them 3–2, and besides, I am chafing in my Toughskins to leave the table.

"Go ahead," my mother says.

My father takes another bite of his tempeh casserole, defeated by the very ideals he has fought to instill in us: independence, high-mindedness, and a respect for due process. "We're raising fascists," he tells my mother.

"That's not strictly true," she says.

"Petty bureaucrats, then," he mutters.

Later that night Clive came to visit me in my bedroom, standing by my window and looking out at the street, flipping through the records that I hadn't thrown out by mistake, finally sitting down on the end of my bed, where I lay on my back, staring at the ceiling. My Toughskins jacket hung from the back of my desk chair. I had abandoned my homework, as usual, to do nothing. Sometimes, a silence existed between us that was hard to break; with other people conversation grew out of a natural desire to know them better, but with my twin, our closest times had been in utero, a time before idle chatter, so we often slipped, Clive and me, into a watery silence. Clive spoke first this time.

"It's easy, you know."

"What's easy?" I asked.

He stood up again and went to the window. That night it seemed as if he was just inquisitive, or after a dramatic effect, but I now know that he was looking for a sign from his pale second-story muse, Faith Crick. "Masturbation."

"I know how to do it. *Jesus.*"

He squinted into the darkness. "Just checking."

"Now would be a good time to leave my room," I told him.

"Your loss, man."

"My gain, pervert."

"I'm only trying to help." A dim light came on across the street, and Clive left me to pursue his sacred love.

I like to think of this time as a flowering, when my abilities as an underachiever, for the very first season, came into full rhododendron bloom. I allowed psychoanalysis, and my free-loving parents, to browbeat me into a deep and prolonged latency, where their furry hands would have no access to my psyche. I became encapsulated, a boy-in-a-plastic-bubble, lost in inner space. We continued to see Dr. Strauss every other week, and when the subject of my masturbatory habits came up, I lied about my object of desire (Faith Crick

on the balance beam, but that might have found its
way back to Clive), and frequency (never, proudly).
Sibyl Strauss, for all of her misconceptions about the
human animal, was no dummy when it came to children, and she suspected me of lying. I brought her a
crumpled tube sock once as an exhibit, but she only
told me sternly, "I'm not interested in your dirty laundry, William." Clive had just recovered a memory,
long before the current rage, and Sibyl had begun
writing a paper on his experience, which she would
deliver in September at a conference in Geneva. From
there she began a lecture tour of Europe, and we never
sat with her again.

As hard as I tried to be the dunce at the Agassiz
School, some special knowledge of geography or flash
of insight on a reading test forever kept me in the
faceless middle of the curve, with fresh immigrants,
and girls with expensive orthodonture. Clive excelled
naturally in the classroom, attentive without being
overeager, raising his hand to answer a teacher's question only if he was certain. The principal saw to it that
we sat in different classes, and the faculty had been
briefed, by a school psychologist, on how to handle our
discrepancies in talent. Only substitutes would call me
Clive by mistake, and as far as I know, no one ever
called him William. If the seventh grade had elected a
president, and recognized a valedictorian, Clive would
have held both offices. He played quarterback on our

flag-football team, captained our basketball team—a
perennial loser—to upset victories over powerhouses
Peabody and Tobin, opened a doubleheader in Little
League by pitching a six-inning no-hitter, while in the
second game he set a league record for putouts in the
outfield (eleven). My athletic career followed an alto-
gether different course: My lack of speed prevented me
from being a factor on the football field, except to fill
the water cooler; when it came to basketball, I was a
point guard without any ball-handling skills, and the
coach called my number only at trash time or when he
needed someone off the bench to draw a charging foul.
My Little League season ended badly—I violated the
laws of physics when, with two men on, two out, in
the bottom of the sixth inning, down by a run, I somehow fouled a pitch back into my left eye-socket, falling
to the ground in a heap. In case you've ever wondered,
home plate is an unforgiving pillow. The last thing I
remember was the degenerate umpire, who knew
nothing about baseball, calling me "out." My freak accident had killed our rally. When I came to, my disappointed teammates had already left the field to be con-
soled by their families, while the opposing team
jumped, cheered, hugged, and otherwise celebrated
their good fortune all around me. I saw my coach kicking his car door in the parking lot. The umpire offered
me a brandy, but I refused. *Life is beautiful,* I thought.
Sealed in a polyester uniform, bleeding from the head,

scorned by friendly Pirates and loved by Indian ene-
mies, I had found rock bottom—or so I thought—the
nadir of my childhood, and I lay there as the afternoon
turned to twilight, enchanted by my failure. Any discussion of my latency period should end here, when I
had reached a perfect state of imperfection, dazed and
bloodied, my cleats mysteriously untied, suspended, for
a moment, between childhood and adolescence. For
now, think of me sitting up with the help of an EMT,
my left eye swollen shut, right eye filled with tears of
gratitude for the pain that life had offered me. An
ambulance had backed onto the baseball diamond and
had drawn a small crowd, licking soft-serve ice cream.
My coach had finished kicking his car, and stood
nearby with the look of a penitent. As I rolled by on
my gurney, the umpire offered him his flask.

"Thanks," my coach said. "Hey, William, buck up,
kid," and then he lied. "Losing doesn't matter."

Have you forgotten that what you are reading is a
kind of diary? That my version of events, as persuasive
as it might seem, is not definitive? Ask my parents:
they are still married, and living in the same rambling
Victorian on Francis Street. Ask Clive: after law school
on the West Coast he returned to Boston and works
long hours as a junior partner at a prestigious law firm
on State Street. He lives in Concord with his new, re-

markable wife, and drives a Saab to work. They are the envy of their neighbors, none of whom are doing badly. As for me, life has been an experiment in trial-and-error, without any guiding principles, or prevailing consolations, a solitary work in progress, like prayer without a God to listen. I have lived in many places (R——, New York; New York City; Boulder, Colorado; San Francisco, California; Portland, Oregon, to name a few) but they are all the same in my jaundiced vision. Small apartments can do that, reduce entire sparkling cities to a catalog of annoyances: footsteps above, cruelty below, traffic, car alarms, and garbage trucks outside the open sliver of a window. I am between degrading jobs, and bad relationships. More often than not I have no money, and I am alone. I hear rumors that my condition is widespread, and I have seen my generation try to make its mark, and fail to come up with anything original. Idiots are happy to be labeled, transformed into a catchphrase or demographic category, but what about the rest of us? I do not take Prozac or any other happy pill, and even if I did, I wouldn't tell you. I have never been in "rehab," or joined a twelve-step recovery program. I do not blame my parents for their small mistakes, or the disappearing comforts of white middle-class privilege, or the torment of growing up with an ideal identical brother. I live my life the way I choose, and if my decisions are sometimes baffling to those who know me, so what? Don't forget, I am proud to be an under-achiever, confirmed by clinical tests and life experi-ence. No one, yet, has changed me, and I predict that no one will.

A word of caution as we move into my adolescence: The private life of a thirteen-year-old underachiever isn't pretty. I had few friends to provide a positive influence, and fewer hobbies to distract me from my pitiful reflection in the mirror. After a shower my hair would grease itself in fifteen minutes, sometimes quicker. My mouth hung open of its own accord. Pim-ples literally erupted. Every night I fought a war against my sex instinct, and it wasn't easy; the rustle of my percale sheets, a window rattling in the wind, the sound of my mother's teacup in its saucer all the way downstairs, any kind of friction at all, sent my mind racing into sexual-fantastic overdrive, draining blood from my extremities to the throbbing locus of my body, the unspeakable, famished soul of teenage boy-hood. Imaginary women beckoned me forward into open arms. Every girl I had ever met—including Dor-othea Zimmerman, my tormenter—wanted a piece of my mincemeat pie, and I was tempted to serve it up. But I taught myself to endure this nightly torture sto-ically, even if, in the end, my unconscious body proved to be far weaker than my conscious one, and led me into a wild orgiastic dream life that relieved the, um, pressure. I often woke up vanquished in the middle of

the night, not to mention sticky, minus a small frac-
tion of my gross national product, and no closer to
knowing nature's secrets than before, when my nightly
ascetic ritual—no touching, please—dulled the instinct
my parents' generation so revered, in the hope, as naive as this may sound, that a solitary exercise of re-
straint might cause a chain reaction, as if a single stop
sign could bring the nation's foul traffic to a halt. How
I fought against their liberation! In my weakest hours,
after catching a glimpse, in a poster rack at the Harvard Coop, of an equestrian Farrah Fawcett riding
bareback in Malibu, or walking home from the public
library with Katie Mulligan, the spit-and-image of
Tatum O'Neal in *Paper Moon*, I followed the example
of Henry Suso, German mystic of the fourteenth cen-
tury (an attractive seminary student—I'll call her "Ju-
lie"—had given Clive a copy of *The Life of the Blessed
Henry Suso* and it somehow found its way into my
floor library), who carried his devotion to absurd
lengths, what we would now call sadomasochism:
rather than smoke the lice from his teeming pallet,
Suso fashioned a pair of torture gloves, covering his
palms with custom-sharpened tacks, and when he
tried, in the middle of the night, to scratch himself, or
brush away a hopping bug, you can imagine what kind
of pleasurable pain resulted. How many times did I
wake up and find my hands clamped around my man-
hood? Don't worry, these veins are empty of any truly

Christian blood, and I came up with a more practical plan for self-deprivation that would keep me from the emergency room at Mount Auburn Hospital. I took out a short-term loan from my eternally liquid brother, more than enough for a trip, one Saturday afternoon, to J. F. Brine Sporting Goods in Harvard Square, where I tried on samples of hockey gloves, all reduced in sticker price for the summer. A legion of tight-lipped, beady-eyed, red-faced Cambridge fathers and their abused, Pee Wee–playing sons kept me company. They had come for the sale, too, and the showroom staff ignored me while they tended to the public spectacle of traditional family values.

"I can't feel my fingers," one boy complained about his pair of Coopers, standing next to a cardboard cut-out of retired Bruin Bobby Orr, who smiled in his uniform.

"Shut up," his father told him. "You'll break 'em in."

"They suck," the boy insisted. "Wicked bad."

"We could try another pair," the salesman offered.

"We'll take 'em," the father announced.

"But, *Dad.*"

"Shut up."

"Dad."

"I said, *shut up.*"

As quickly as possible I chose the cheapest pair of gloves I could find, and took my place in line behind our favorite family. They bonded with a cruel chuckle over my purchase ("Check bait," the father commented, pointing at me with his thumb) and hurried out with a shopping bag to meet the New England boiled dinner waiting for them at five o'clock. The cashier, too, had a little trouble with my scrawny presence in this shrine to health and violence, and I endured his condescension, then went off to spend the rest of my life savings on comic books, and a beefburger deluxe at the Brigham's lunch counter.

I will spare you, diary, any further descriptions of the nocturnal goings-on in my bedroom, only to say that hockey gloves, in the short term, are an effective deterrent to tenderness of any kind, should you ever need it. In the long run, however, leatherette proved to be no match for my peaking hormone levels, and soon I had a chafing problem.

I can see now that it was out of desperation, in a last-ditch attempt, I believe, to avoid the "fairer sex" and extend my happy latency, that I somehow convinced my parents to enroll me at a private boys' school in a nearby suburb. For reasons that will soon become clear, I will hereafter refer to this institution of lower learning as the Boys' Prison. The four years I spent there passed in a blur of Latin translations, fetal animal dissections, forced exercise, terrible meals spiked with saltpeter, and the ritual abuse of weaker boys. I'll admit to being wooed, at first, by the rolling, impossibly green chapel lawn in the middle of the campus, and the bright white Greek Revival meetinghouse itself, shipped in pieces from somewhere in Virginia to preside over the playing fields, and to fill the windows of the stuffy academic buildings with a view of its stately facade. Every weekday morning the pews in the chapel creaked with the energy of three hundred sullen minimen in matching ties and jackets, listening to Mr. Hanson play, on the rusty organ, overdramatized interpretations of Bach, Brahms, and Haydn, with an occasional rendition of something more patriotic and fanciful, like "Over There." I fought off sleep through countless speeches by the headmaster, known affectionately as "The Wimp," a spineless frog of a man with a gift for turning language into something dull and ordinary, and for this, more than anything else, I can never forgive him—or any of my other dangerously earnest guards and wardens. Strike that: The Wimp was just trying to make a living for his family, and we were children of obscene privilege, deserving of nothing better. My distracted, quasi-Bohemian family had nothing to do with the untrampled chapel lawn, the terraced playing fields and their fresh-drawn boundary lines, white stripes decreed by God, it seemed, and the campus pathways, between periods, crowded with little businessmen-in-training, lurching hockey players, football linemen, future doctors and lawyers, all carrying the same maroon book bag with our school's proud symbol on the side, an extended telescope. Did this mean we were provided with the tools to enhance our vision? Hardly.

The Boys' Prison specialized in educating athletes for a certain future at an Ivy League college, just enough to justify their scholarships, not enough to question how their parents came into so much easy money, or to give them pause in the middle of a date rape. To the Prison's credit, this is a subtle balance to strike. Teenagers are easily distracted by their hormones, and as a reward for our daily privations, twice a semester they organized grim DJ-driven mixers with inmates from a local Girls' Prison, some of whom didn't mind being smeared with sticky punch in a darkened squash court. A "game" specimen was easy to identify: The "nice" girls hated her openly, the chaperons watched her every movement, and later, after she had managed to slip away from the dance floor and return unnoticed, careful observation found a certain tousle to her hair, and a telltale unfastening of her bra strap. She was my soul mate, but I never spoke to her. I pursued mythical, unattainable girls who saw right through me, scrawny pilgrim at the altar, to the towering left wing with a chipped front tooth that told the story of a winning goal at the New England Championships, and who kept a VHS tape at home, for those romantic moments, of his arthroscopic knee surgery. Once again the homely girls would flock to my side, responding to my wan outsider look, and I had to keep moving to avoid them. I was handsome, I suppose, but that was underneath a film of grease, and forehead boils. Did I want a glass of punch? Not really. Did I want to dance? Never. Did I want to go for a walk in the squash courts? Only in the service of a greater hunger, to follow rustling skirts, to be near, in the shadows, pearline shoulders, and gorgeous, insistent whispers of *no*.

Clive opted for public school to the delight of my parents, an experimental program at Cambridge Rindge and Latin High School called Pilot, where classes, it seemed, were optional, and the female-to-male ratio hovered around three to two. Not that it mattered to him: Clive's second-story flirtation with Faith Crick had escalated into a very public relationship, making them our neighborhood's First Couple. Clive tied up our phone line with endless calls, spent hours composing love notes, which he hand-delivered to her door, walked with her the length of Francis Street to the Divinity School and back again almost every night, passing underneath my lonely window. They talked seriously and never laughed, like an Amish couple, and their public displays of affection, unlike those of most teenage lovers, were limited to a kiss good-night on her front porch, unless Mr. Crick was smoking his pipe on the porch swing—then Clive stole a kiss behind a hedge and left her at the end of the walk, waving good-night from a distance. In private, according to Clive, they were more like rabbits, and I found their discretion, which must have been difficult, admirable. At the very beginning of our adolescence our parents took an active interest in our sexuality, buying us the latest guidebooks and oral histories to ensure a guilt-free initiation, but now that Clive had become a practicing fornicator, they left him alone, and turned their attention to latent me, leaving pamphlets on my pillow about safe and effective birth-control, and encouraging me to spend time with the Happy Couple, so that I might learn a thing or two about the mysteries of young women.

Faith had no ordinary twin sister to offer me. Because of her perfection, the popular girls at school, apparently, could be cruel to her, and her generous aura attracted just the sort of awkward follower I struggled to avoid. I was rude and sullen company, I'm afraid. On Faith's front porch one night in late October I rejected the advances of Alma Mueller, who wore cutoff jeans so tight around her cellulitic rump that she would be hospitalized, later that year, for a blood clot. Alma smashed my pumpkin (we were carving jack-o'-lanterns for Halloween) and ran off into the night. Underneath a tree on the grounds of the Divinity School I failed to kiss Missy Aronson, a submissive girl with shingles (chronic pain informed the corners of her smile). She hated me quietly, and refused my offer to walk her home.

My worst trespass on hallowed ground took place in March, at a kissing party in Faith's bedroom where, during our two minutes together in a darkened closet, I lost contact with bookworm Sarabeth Malarkey, and when she opened the door prematurely, I was found in an embrace with the very leotard Faith had worn on the balance beam the day I fell in love with her. My lame attempts at an explanation failed. Sarabeth, whose father was a therapist, diagnosed me with a mild form of fetishism. At that point I was merely a day inmate at the Boys' Prison, free to go home after an hour of bootcamp-style intramural sports. The kissing party so embarrassed me, however, that I could no longer bear the temptations of our neighborhood, and the next year, despite numerous heated discussions, straw votes, and a parental filibuster that lasted throughout the month of July, I returned to the Prison as a boarding student.

Let me be clear that I am against the unnatural separation of male and female human animals. We are all fraternal, and in possession of the same vital organs—brain for thinking, heart for pumping, lungs for breathing, et cetera—and even though our reproductive roles are sometimes adversarial, we are complementary products, and depend on one another for survival. There are some, of course, who prefer their own reflection in the heart-shaped mirror; others, like nuns and celibate priests, prefer their intimacy spiritual; there are hermits in shacks in subway tunnels, and spinsters who live alone; even so, sex, religion, and solitude are small condolences to me, simple answers to greater questions of identity: Am I really here? Where is *here*, anyway? If you leave me, will I disappear? Simplified, I know, but remember that I am, in all things, an underachiever, bound by nature to wrestle with the dull unanswerable and then give up, to the benefit of no one.

During my first year as an overnight inmate at the Boys' Prison I lived in Underbelly (my invention), a brick Federal cell-block for unwanted, unloved sons of local politicians, bankers, doctors, and entrepreneurs. We were overseen by an insane faculty member who lived with his frightened family in an apartment next door with walls so thin we heard everything, even his children's nightly prayers for deliverance. Mr. Sullivan (I have chosen his fictive name carefully—the Mr. Sullivans in my home state are outnumbered only by their constipated sons, usually named Jim, and always nicknamed "Sully") began his abuse in the morning by screaming at his wife about the state of the apartment, a tirade that ended with the distant ringing of the chapel bell, summoning all of us to morning services. Bleary eyed, overstuffed from my breakfast of starch and mild tranquilizers, I would often stumble out of Underbelly to see, among the traffic of boys crossing the chapel lawn from every direction, Mr. Sullivan leading his wife, still in a nightgown, by the hand to a glacial boulder, where they ducked into the hidden shadows, to do what, I didn't know. A few minutes later he emerged on the other side, alone, barking orders to the younger boys: "Pull up that tie!" "Get a haircut, Bobby, you look like a prom queen!" "Say good-morning to your elders, or else!"

I had a roommate that year, Clarkson Boyd, a slow learner with custom-made shirts, alligator loafers, and a gold-plated money clip to hold his enormous allowance. Boyd, as we called him, rarely spoke, and he ate candy steadily. At night we would lie awake in our beds, listening to another one of Mr. Sullivan's tantrums. I should have called 911, but we didn't have a phone, and my punishment would have been potentially life threatening. In the room next door Marky O'Leary, an orphan hockey phenom in constant search of sleep, would punch his pillow and groan.

"Sullivan's bad tonight," I remarked once to Boyd. "What is it, midnight?"

Boyd took the lollipop out of his mouth for a second. "Maybe he'll punch out a window. Glass everywhere, like."

"You'd enjoy that, wouldn't you."

"Wicked, like."

"Asshole," Marky said out loud next door.

At times like this I thought of home, not out of any longing or premature nostalgia, but out of envy, almost, that Clive should be there in his bedroom sleeping soundly, and his dreams, once so troubled, would be softened by the last thing he had heard that night, Faith's voice on her Princess telephone. Something hit the wall, hard, and Mr. Sullivan stopped yelling.

"Finally," Boyd said, and rolled over, sucking on his lollipop.

I laid my head down on the rubber mattress, and covered my head with my flimsy pillow. *If there is a God,* I thought, *He will bring a plague here.*

The next year I barely graduated from Underbelly to Sparrow Hall, the "idyllic" dormitory for upperclassmen—at least that's how the school catalog described the Georgian ruin without hot running water where I endured the next two years of my Spartan existence. All the same, Sparrow constituted a real step up: single rooms with a view of the playing fields, a pay phone, and a master with no family to bully after hours. Mr. Stocking (too fake? It captures his nylon essence, anyway), a confirmed bachelor, ran a very loose ship in some ways, giving us free rein until lights-out at eleven, unless we disturbed his alcoholic drinking with our horseplay. During the day a sober

Mr. Stocking taught Psychology, of which he was a stunted victim, Ethics, which eluded him, and coached gland cases and their lightweight sycophants in Varsity Wrestling. At night he slipped into something more comfortable, usually a satin bathrobe, and drank Cosmopolitans in his sitting room. Seniors, occasionally, were invited in to watch John Wayne pictures behind closed doors. When the enemy died, they cheered wildly, and stomped on the floor.

Pause and reflect for a moment: an all-boys' dormitory, with no parents or young women within a two-mile radius to provide a civilizing influence. They could have spiked our sloppy joes with laudanum in the dining hall, and Sparrow still would have been a zoo. My blockmates followed a variety of profane traditions, like "submarining," which involved balancing from a two-by-six set across the top of a bathroom stall, and sh—ing down into the toilet from that lofty seat (forgive me the imagery). The submariner's aim is crucial, of course, although the occasional miss could be a real crowd-pleaser.

In this atmosphere only the most freakish talents received positive reinforcement. Pollard "Fred" Baker, my next door neighbor at Sparrow, ate noxious combinations of food in the dining hall for big money. Among the many who considered themselves flatulence musicians, Arthur Wheelwright was Igor Stravinsky and, like a prop comedian, carried with him at

all times, in his book bag, a changing assortment of
sight gags—I remember a lighter, a shining silver pin-
wheel, and a referee's whistle, but the truth is, I would
like to forget almost everything I saw during my im-
prisonment. A senior named Edward Flynn garnered
the most popularity at Sparrow for his own special talent: picking up objects between the cheeks of his . . .
you know what I mean, and nearly every night, after
dinner and mandatory study hall in the library, we
would gather in his dorm room for an exhibition. My
blockmates took turns presenting him with belongings
to lift, which Edward would turn over in his hands
and weigh carefully, considering all the factors that
went into a perfect "grip." I saw him lift ski boots, a
clock radio, an extension lamp, two-liter Coke bottles
both empty and full, a potted plant, textbooks. I even
saw him lift a toolbox once, to gasps of astonishment.
Edward stripped down to his boxer shorts in order to
perform, crouched over the object like a sumo wrestler,
lowered himself down, squeezed hard, lifted, and, more
often than not, raised his arms in victory. Every night
a standing ovation. I could have made things easier on
myself by participating, but I honestly didn't want the
few things I owned anywhere near Edward Flynn's
boxer shorts, and whenever it was my turn to chal-
lenge him, I balked. The honor my fellow inmates saw
in this foul baptism was lost on me.

"What's the matter," Edward would ask, "are you a

pussy or something?" The crowd turned on me, seeming to agree. "Fred" Baker was inspecting his shaving mirror, which Edward had lifted on his first try.

"Not a scratch," he said. "Jesus, that's talent."

"Don't you think it's kind of *unsanitary*?" I asked lamely.

Lucky for me a surprise inspection by Mr. Stocking prevented any violence, but as the crowd broke up I heard it from the seniors.

"Fag," Edward called me.

"Leatherboy," said Arthur Wheelwright.

"Dimwit." That was Simeon Hurwitz, football player, who hired an English exchange student to take his SATs.

Ashish Rapathaswamy, a future early-round departure from Wimbledon, uttered a withering "Queer." For the rest of the week they would make animal noises whenever I was in their vicinity.

On weekend furlough I would rejoin my family already in progress, like a television series, confused by their interactions, dazed by my passage from the Boys' Prison to a place so dissimilar. Ronald Reagan's first inauguration as president had turned my disappointed parents bitter, especially my father, who retreated into his study for most of the Great Communicator's first term, coming out to mutter about the Evil Empire speech, the paranoid ramblings of cabinet secretaries Haig and Watt, and anything having to do with the

Constitution-hating attorney general Edwin Meese.
We didn't really see him again until the Iran-Contra
hearings; by that time I was away at college, and Clive
had moved into a four-person suite at Eliot House,
across Harvard Yard from our quickly gentrifying
neighborhood.

My mother maintained a more practical interest in
our lives, and every semester around tuition time she
interrogated me about persistent rumors surrounding
the Boys' Prison—secret hate societies, corporal punishment—and assured me that if I wanted to drop out
and go to public school with Clive, both she and my
father would support my decision. "What is it," she
asked me once, clearly exasperated, "that you *like*
about the place?" I gave her some lame answer about
the facilities and my "classical" education, which was
really pseudo- at best (in her company I once made
reference to Ecclesiastes as if he were a Greek play-
wright), and to her credit she always abided by my
foolish wish to stay. If I had all that money back now,
not that it was mine to spend, I would sooner burn it
in a pile than hand it over to those missionary blood-
suckers. Still, if my destiny, predetermined by God,
nature, or my environment, was to become not just a
garden-variety underachiever but a great one, then
squandering my youth at the Boys' Prison was a rare
and perfect opportunity, and I wouldn't waste it. Noth-

ing bountiful would ever grow in fields so righteously salted.

Only a well-adjusted twin brother could recognize how desperate my situation was, and since my academic life was clearly a lost cause, Clive tried his best to introduce me to the wonderment of teenage love, setting me up with more of Faith's bizarre followers, at least the few who hadn't heard of my habitually bad dating conduct. We were sixteen now, and Clive already had his driver's license; I had failed my first driving test by swerving to avoid a squirrel on Massachusetts Avenue, swerving back to dodge a pedestrian, and clipping the open driver's door of an illegally parked car, all of which also earned me a ticket for reckless driving. Now that Clive was mobile, anyway, he and Faith had discovered all the choice romantic spots in Cambridge and beyond, bringing me along with whoever my date was, girls too lonely to stay at home on yet another Friday night, and who didn't mind finding themselves in the backseat of a yellow Subaru with a sullen stranger, pimples and all.

I will not describe what time had done to Faith, only to say that it had been kind to her, and cruel to everyone who didn't see his love for her returned. Like every good soul who is blessed with something unbelievable to others, Clive had no idea how rare she was, and only later, when they had broken things off for the last time during a snowy Christmas break from college, did he appreciate the full extent of her enchanting presence. Warm, intelligent, beautiful, kind—in some parallel universe where reality meets our aspirations for it, every teenage girl is headstrong Faith, and every boy is humble Clive.

I had resolved that year to grow up a little, and in our Subaru, parked just down the street in a secluded parking lot on the grounds of the Divinity School, I traded kisses with a nervous redhead whose name eludes me, though I can remember the exact geometry of the freckles on her face, and her slender neck with its black hole of a scab, a bug bite, and, believe it or not, her ankles, smudged with dirt from wearing flip-flops, one of which she lost that first night. We met on three successive weekends before I lost my mind and told her that I loved her. We were parked outside the Store 24 on Broadway. "Thanks," she said as Faith came back and handed her an Orange Crush, *to match her hair*, I thought, and when she kept her distance in the back, singing along with the radio, I returned to my unhappy self, frowning out the window at the stupid traffic, cursing myself for having revealed my true feelings.

Similar experiments followed, some more physically involved, others less, while Faith and Clive, modest as always, left us alone in the car to find one of their many secret hideaways. A single night stands out as a kind of paradigm: Clive had discovered a nine-hole golf course on the shores of Fresh Pond, and more specifically, a hole in the chain-link fence around the perimeter big enough to crawl through, undetected, in the dark. My date for our foursome that Friday, Mary-Kate Fernandes, knew Faith from AP English class, and shared her love of Herman Melville. I had skimmed *Moby-Dick* that year in search of the erotic parts—a disappointing enterprise, unless you count Ishmael and Queequeg's first night together at the Spouter-Inn. We talked about the inconsolable Captain Ahab and his obsession with the milky-white Leviathan, and Mary-Kate came to the conclusion that he could have benefited from attending a support group with other members of the buccaneer community. I didn't mind her braces—they were on her legs, of course, and rattled suggestively, I thought, on our way across the fairway to a scenic water hazard, where real swans mixed with metal decoys, pockmarked with pellet-gun fire. Mary-Kate limped along in the moonlight. At that point I had accepted my fate to live among the homely, or crippled, or slightly disturbed, and I had just begun to see the grace in human imperfection, whether the ultimate cause turned out to be the lottery of genetics or the more traditional original sin. When I looked at Mary-Kate that night, really looked at her, I noticed that her eyes were shallow and guarded, as if a curtain had been drawn before her

inmost thoughts, out of modesty, perhaps, or to protect
her from a world that only saw her for her subtle
difference from the "norm." She stopped to adjust a
Velcro strap below her knee. Clive and Faith had
reached the water's edge, and seemed to be heading
for a storage shed on the far side of the pond, nestled
in the bushes. "If you want," she told me, "you can go
ahead." Her cardigan sweater hung open, showing off
a pretty floral dress and the clear beginnings of a figure.

"I'll wait," I said.

"I don't need your help, if that's what you're getting
at."

I heard crickets, and traffic on the nearby parkway.
"Why would you need my help?"

Mary-Kate straightened up and started walking
again. "I'm just saying."

We chose a short par three with a slight dogleg to
the left, settling down at the ladies' tee, which had a
nicer view of the fairway in the moonlight. Mary-Kate
loosened her braces and laid her legs out flat. She
asked, and I told her about life at the Boys' Prison, the
airless classrooms, my moronic classmates, the British-
style homoerotic regimentation, more than I had ever
confessed to anyone about my life there. She gasped,
laughed at the absurdity, made faces when I described
the goings-on at Sparrow Hall. Then I asked her about
her own life, and she launched into a story about her

local crusade for handicapped entrances at every city school, which inspired me.

"I've kissed lots of boys," she said out of the blue.

"I've kissed lots of girls, but then they reject me."

She buttoned her cardigan against the chill. "I just don't think I'm ready for a serious relationship. Not until I'm twenty, at least."

We sat there in the moonlight for a while, listening to an artificial stream trickle across the fairway below us. My heart was full with her, but I lacked the means to express myself, other than the usual words, and tender actions, which seemed like inherited wisdom to me, universal LOVE, the failing panacea of my parents' generation: flower children, baby boomers, whatever name you'd like to use. Exactly what had the sexual revolution gained them, after all? Some measure of bodily happiness, a sex instinct unfettered, the herpes virus, the social acceptability of T-shirts and cutoff shorts, but what else? Had they really changed our values and attitudes? And there I was, on a golf course at midnight with a girl I really liked, underachieving all over again in a misguided attempt to *make it new,* and pioneer a romantic avant-garde where nothing started, in the moonlight, would ever finish, and the greatest love, or kiss, would be the one that never grew beyond its promising beginning; that way no one would ever have to live with an imperfect lover's guilt when things came to an end, as they do, inevitably.

"I have to go," I said, standing up.

Mary-Kate looked confused for a second, and then what must have been a familiar, hardened look befell her face. "I'll meet you at the car," she said, tightening her braces.

I let her believe the worst of me, and left.

That night, as I lay in bed, I saw for the first time in its entirety the lonely road ahead, and I felt exhilarated. No one would ever know me. No one would think of me first thing in the morning, call me to fill an empty afternoon, sit beside me in a movie theater and shudder, for a second, when I slipped my hand over the soft skin on the inside of a knee, remembering a deep caress. I would reject real love, and frown on human tenderness. This was my plan, anyway, and like all the others I have made, it would end in failure. I have fallen in love, however misdirected, known sexual obsession (does it count if she never met me?), and felt my love returned by more than a few women, if only briefly. I have knelt and prayed halfheartedly for my survival, so that I might, in my own circuitous fashion, come face to face with happiness. The seminarian in me would ask *What does God think?* As if He would ever care about a nameless wanderer among His baptized children. As if my disease were real, and not invented.

III. Adulthood for Beginners

When I undertook this diary I made a promise not to form my recollections into something easily digested, some cloying testimonial to my resilience in the face of small adversities, or a bildungsroman bittersweet with life, love, and heartbreak, or even a confession in the religious sense, my paltry imitation of a young St. Augustine wrestling with his conversion and the meaning of his faith. Like the onetime logician from Hippo I have stolen pears and wasted them, sat under fig trees

and heard things spoken in the air, and still I am uncertain about God's existence. Belief, after all, is impossible for an underachiever. Augustine enjoyed long
years as a skeptic, arguing with the Manicheans in
Carthage, indulging Alypius in his trips to the Coli-
seum in Rome—his pseudoscientific treatise *Beauty
and Proportion*, which sought to measure, in units, the
source of physical attraction, is the underachiever's
model text, especially since he lost the completed
manuscript. If Augustine had stopped there, unfulfilled
and bitter, Christianity might well have been completely different. This is idle speculation, of course, but
without a reliable figment of His face just overhead,
what else is there? Conspiracy theories, rumors, and
entertaining myths on television, countless little dia-
ries far more lurid than this. My fondest wish, then,
would be for my diary to end up in the hands of someone in better circumstances than my own, the mature
Augustine with his letters already in wide circulation,
a happy celebrity or wildly successful businessman,
just so they might remember what it was like before
God's lightning struck and the very air, the paparazzi
and all the number-crunching minions shouted their
names out loud for everyone to hear.

I am a humble man with despotic tendencies. I am
a saint with the lifestyle of a sinner, or do I mean the
opposite, a sinner who has unrequited, saintlike aspirations, no, wait—as you can see, I am still in the thick

of it. Please, do not confuse this diary with a memoir written for a therapeutic purpose, designed to exorcize my demons and provide a thrill for everyone who cares to watch them all take flight, *Look, he's telling secrets;* I am no different now, more than halfway through these mostly happy recollections, than I was the moment I began to write them down. I am not lounging on an offshore island with my profits, nor am I, for that matter, serving time in prison. I am an ordinary man. If you want to locate me in time and space, good luck. My address is unknown, my phone number unlisted. My family knows where I am, of course, but they've been given explicit instructions not to reveal my whereabouts to ex-friends, ex-girlfriends, creditors, missionaries, secret admirers, law-enforcement agencies, the IRS, and, last but not least, hypothetical readers of this document.

It is purely for pedagogical purposes that I include my college years in the "adulthood" section of my diary. Strictly speaking, I was still an adolescent when I enrolled, under duress, at R—— College in upstate New York, and when I finally graduated cum laude five years later due to rampant grade inflation, I had scarcely matured any further, despite the twenty or so pounds I had gained in the interim. (A steady diet of beer and chicken wings has been proven to retard human progress—look at the population of Buffalo, New York. The bars are open late, serving pitchers and dollar buckets, but who lives there, other than some of the finest angioplasty specialists in the United States? Everyone else is drunk, a dentist, or a professional professional-football fan, with a few unhappy exceptions.) I had applied to other, better schools, and found disappointment in their flimsy return envelopes, although one college that had already accepted Clive placed me on the waiting list, out of pity, I suspected.

Because I had applied from the Boys' Prison, with test scores just lower than Louis Liu, our class valedictorian and already a part-time research chemist at Squibb, R—— College had plied me with weekly mailings and phone calls from a bubbly admissions counselor, who made suggestive promises. Don't believe what you've heard, she told me, about the eight-month winters. The female-to-male ratio, she claimed, was climbing. As for the facilities, most of the improvement projects were nearly completed, and the ice storm I may have read about in the papers hadn't limbed *every* tree on campus, so by the time I arrived there in September, communication lines with the outside world would once again be open. *Please deposit sixty cents,* an automated operator added. *Thank you.* I had no other offers, and I accepted.

My family made the drive upstate with me on a sweltering day in the middle of August, one that I remember not for its educational significance, because

my father's station wagon didn't have air condition-
ing, and Mitterrand, our second golden Labrador (after Castro my parents had become more pragmatic),
nearly died of heat stroke in back. We hosed him
down in the parking lot of some nameless burger joint
on the Thruway, underneath a sky about to burst. The
dried grass crackled in the highway's breeze. Birds fell
from the trees, which prompted my mother to call the
Audubon Society, and they assured her no significant
species were threatened. Clive bought us Popsicles,
which melted in our hands, and we took turns coax-
ing Mitterrand back to life with a soggy cheese-
burger. "Breathe," my mother said, obvious but good
advice, especially for a socialist. Once his tail was
safely wagging again, we set off for school in haste,
trying to make my freshman orientation at four
o'clock.

Sure, the campus, when we finally arrived, late,
may have been in the middle of a few construction
projects, and the trees—all of them—might have been
denuded by the ice storm, and perhaps the river that
meandered on the southern border was the only green
thing there, stinking to high heaven. My classmates, it
seemed, had all arrived on time, and wandered
through the dirt and rubble smiling like idiots, name
tags affixed to their COED NAKED FRISBEE T-shirts. Maybe
some of my peers, to keep things simple, would leave

their name tags stuck to their shirts all through the first semester and, instead of introducing themselves at a keg party, would point to the tag and say "Me." I'll admit, the admissions counselor who met my family that first day should have tipped me off, the one I had been talking to for months, who turned out to be a junior psychology major and vice-president of her sorority, as well as a believer that sweatpants, if worn baggy enough, and matched with a sweatshirt that extended to the knees, are not only appropriate wardrobe for a business meeting but can hide the ill effects of nightly pizza binges. I should have known that first day on campus, but didn't, that a wasteland like this would be the perfect place to spend my college years, all five of them, alienated, as I would be, from the mainstream, unrecognized by other underachievers who might be lurking in the bowels of the Student Union. From the first my parents cast a skeptical eye on my alma mater, and after the admissions counselor had left us in my tiny double room to attend a pledge meeting, they read through my student handbook to check her facts. Yes, the main library held only a hundred thousand volumes, and some of these were water damaged. Yes, many of the classes were taught by student aides, and when the supply of free instructors had been exhausted, they called in substitute teachers from the public school system. As Clive put it, "This place is a joke." But my parents let me stay, and I didn't argue.

So I set out in cheap beer country to become a man. I remember standing outside the dormitory with my roommate, Wendell McTeague, a fake Australian, watching my parents drive away. The dog barked silently at a jackhammer breaking the sidewalk into pieces. Behind us a dump truck started beeping in reverse, carrying dirt away from an excavation. Safety-orange fences boxed the landscape.

"Good riddance," Wendell said, still waving. "Now we can find some sheilas."

I had recently purchased a thirty-six pack of condoms in anticipation of the liberties I might enjoy outside the Boys' Prison. Wendell, too, had bought a healthy supply, and he immediately set about trying to use them. He kept a careful count, saving and filing all the wrappers, and on Sunday mornings, as I suffered in bed from crippling hangovers, Wendell would stroll in wearing his full-length duster, pull a condom wrapper from his pocket, and say, "Eleven, mate," or whatever number he had reached in his goal of two hundred and thirteen, or every decent-looking girl, he had figured mathematically, on campus. His project sickened me. I avoided the thick-ankled coeds who followed me to the dining hall after class, and as for the few I admired, I inundated them with love notes and borrowed poetry. "Bouquet of Belle Scavoir," by Wallace Stevens, was my favorite, a gorgeous meditation on earthly beauty that both surpassed their reading level, and struck them as creepy. "It is she that he wants," the poet writes, "to look at directly,/ Someone before him to see and to know."

What a lie! I only wanted them to sleep with me, as love starved as I felt coming out of my extended latency. I wanted to forget, for a moment, that I was born to be an outcast, the downside of my brother's brilliance and personality, a negative example for everyone, even the mongoloid fraternity brothers who let me into their keg parties because they had to under campus bylaws, stamping my hand with GEEK in bright red ink.

In December, at a theme party with a meaning that escaped me, mashed between Wendell, six-feet-four in his duster and outback boots, and his best friend Sam, an androgynous Filipino from New Jersey, I locked eyes with a girl I had never seen before, obviously drunk, pressed against a wall while three fraternity brothers took turns blowing in her ear. Was she pretty? I have always had a "thing" for tears and mascara. At that moment she was trying, unsuccessfully, to untangle a wad of chewing gum from her hair. She looked at me, shrugged her shoulders out of her party dress, and handed her empty beer cup to one of the brothers, which he replaced immediately. I looked away, embarrassed by our intimate moment.

"Thirty-one," Wendell wrongly predicted.

As her chaperons for the evening lifted her above their heads and carried her through the crowd, then up the stairs to their bunk room, I knew, somehow, that I had just seen someone who would be significant in the coming months, or years, the kind of woman who might tolerate my presence, just as I would learn to appreciate her endless drinking, and promiscuity, and bask in every sleepless night these problems brought me, every snicker behind my back, every story whispered in the empty library about a freshman girl named Natalie who cheated on her boyfriend on weekends, then came to her senses and confessed to God on Sunday morning, and to the stooge who loved her on Sunday afternoon, and the thing is, he always forgave her, *can you believe it?* I am not proud of my stupidity in matters of the heart. But I can tell you that I loved her earnestly, even as I knew, from the very beginning, that she would torture me, and I would mean nothing to her in the end—another set of hands to hold her beer, a mattress to come home to late at night, someone reliable, in the morning, to help her piece her night together, and listen to her dreams.

I spoke to Clive on the phone every week, and we filled each other in on our college experiences, which couldn't have been more divergent. Clive lived in a suite with three other high achievers, one the son of a senior senator from Alabama; one the youngest son of a hipster journalist whom our parents had long admired for his early gonzo work; the last a direct descendant of Teddy Roosevelt, who was a little slow, apparently, but sweet. Clive found his classes less difficult than he had expected, and had plenty of time to socialize with his growing circle of future leaders.

I would call him at night, after I had spent my half hour at the library, and before Wendell and I would order our nightly bucket of fifty Buffalo wings, extra celery and blue cheese. Faith had broken his heart by going away to the University of California at Berkeley, but at that point they were still together, talking late at night (for him) and writing daily letters, which he sometimes read to me over the phone. I still envied him their relationship, as lonely as I was, and though I carried the same torch for Faith, its flame was flickering or, rather, burned for both of them now. Clive had been in love with her for so long that I couldn't imagine him with anybody else, and together they had always been so kind to me, and understanding of my sullen ways; as unaccustomed as I was to noble feelings, I wanted them to make it. I encouraged Clive over the phone, telling him, "She'll never do any better than you."

Across the room Wendell performed his nightly exercises in his underwear, an allegedly Australian calisthenic I had never seen before.

"Thanks," Clive said, "I know that." Chet Baker sang "Just Friends" in the background, and one of Clive's roommates improvised along with the record, softly, on an upright piano. "It's just that she's so far away, and everybody in California, it sounds like, is asking her out to dinner."

"That's nothing new," I said.

Wendell had started counting out loud to his exercises, and Clive asked, "What is he, an arithmetic major?"

I covered the phone and asked Wendell, "Keep it down, will you?"

"Fuck off, mate," he said.

"Exercises," I explained to Clive. His suitemate abandoned Chet Baker for an even more sophisticated Nina Simone. Across a gaping hole in the courtyard outside my window (water main problems), one of my neighbors had stuck his stereo speakers outside to proclaim his love for Billy Joel. I tried to close my window before Clive could hear "Movin' Out."

"So, what are Harvard girls like up close?"

"I'm not looking," Clive answered, leaving the phone for a second while another suitemate handed him a mixed drink, crushed ice rattling in his highball. "Cheers," Clive said. "Honus makes the best mint julep." He took a long sip and asked, "What about the girls up there?"

Wendell had progressed to the second stage of his workout program, wiping his underarms dry with paper towels. "They're kind of overweight, mostly."

"Sorry, man."

"That's all right," I said. "I've got lots of work I should be doing." I had a term paper due in political philosophy, though I hadn't found the classroom yet, and a makeup exam in chemistry—multiple choice, so at least I had a chance.

"There isn't anyone you like?"

"Well," I answered, hesitant to mention Natalie, whom I hadn't started seeing yet. I had spent the past week wandering around campus during daylight hours (a mistake, I later learned) in a fruitless search for her, "there's one, I guess, but I'm not sure."

Clive wished me luck, and told me he had to go. "There's a party at Hasty Pudding," he explained. "Those guys are crazy."

"Tell Faith I miss her."

Clive's chipped ice rattled as he finished his drink. "I'll tell her," he said, forgetting his promise immediately, I was sure of it. "Honus, I'm thirsty."

My courtship with Natalie, if you can call it that, began over a malfunctioning beer tap at a party the following weekend. How did I recognize her? She was wearing the same party dress, which, upon closer inspection later that night, appeared not to have been washed since I first saw her. She had cut the chewing gum out of her shoulder-length hair with a scissors, leaving a bald patch behind one ear that I would discover with trembling fingers. Early on the party had been crowded, filling the rooms of a suite in Concrete Jungle, a Le Corbusier—inspired high-rise dormitory for upperclassmen, luxurious accommodations at our underfunded school. I had spent an hour plastered to the bars of a grated window, a common feature of rooms above the second floor, which had been installed to protect students from the rational urge, in those parts, to jump. But something had gone wrong with the beer supply, and the party quickly emptied, leaving me, the bewildered hosts, who had started to clean up with lawn-and-leaf bags, and Natalie, who refused to believe the beer tap had actually broken, or even worse, the keg was dry. I saw my opportunity and took it, approaching her with my plastic cup outstretched. Heavy drinkers, in their own way, are touchingly optimistic when it comes to liquor. NyQuil? Delicious. Lysol? An acquired taste, but refreshingly piquant to enthusiasts. My cup, in Natalie's eyes, was more than just half full, it was a godsend. I took the sputtering tap from her hand, put it down on the dented keg, and handed her my chalice.

"Thanks," she said. "I hate it when there's no more beer."

The riot in the elevators had, at last, subsided, and everything was quiet. I thought for sure that she could hear my heart beating in wild, irregular thumps.

"In my room I have a twelve-pack of Old Milwaukee."

Already, she had downed my first offering. "Wow, you're nice."

Natalie may not have been the perfect woman, but I was not the perfect man. Yes, she turned out to be an unpredictable girlfriend, prone to short disappearances, broken dates, and lapses of memory that included my name. The benefits of her company, however, ranged from drunken visits in the middle of the night, even though Wendell, a jerk in every aspect, wouldn't give us any privacy, and complained if we started fooling around, to amorous adventures in the library stacks, such as they were. At least no one ever used them, or so we thought, until one night in the biography section when Natalie's elbow dislodged a Carlos Baker and I came face to face with the single unblinking eye of a curious work-study student, searching through the lower stacks, probably, for young lovers at a third-rate university who had found a practical purpose for the outdated and mostly disintegrating volumes. "Hey," Natalie said when I suddenly stopped researching her cervix, "what gives?" Our Peeping Tom slid the Baker back in Dewey decimal order, and took off down the aisle. I mumbled an apology and tried, with some difficulty, to find my place. "Hurry up," she said. "Happy Hour starts in fifteen minutes."

Natalie showed flashes of brilliance, however, like the time, having heard of Wendell's outrageous sexual claims, she watched him strike out continually at a party, and convinced me to follow him, at a safe distance, to see just where he would sleep that night. Sure enough, Wendell's nightmare ended at Sam the Filipino's room. "At least he sort of *looks* like a girl," Natalie told me. I wasn't convinced that Sam actually had all the masculine equipment, and remained neutral on the subject of Wendell's sexual preference. It was his own business, at any rate, and the next morning when he stumbled home, sneered at Natalie, and pronounced "Forty-seven," I felt for him. We refrained from offering our stolen knowledge, a decision which I don't regret. Soon the first Crocodile Dundee movie would expose him as a fraud, and Wendell hung up his duster to go underground, disappearing for a semester abroad in England. Unfortunately, he returned a fake skinhead who insisted on calling french fries "chips," and enjoyed yelling "Wot!" across the student center.

One more moment or two with Natalie, and then I will move on. I took her home for Thanksgiving our sophomore year, and we spent the weekend looking, unsuccessfully, for a bar in Cambridge that stayed open after midnight. Clive took us on a tour of Harvard ("I like all the bricks," Natalie said. "Are they real?"), but mostly he reunited with Faith, who had flown back from Berkeley to see him. The four of us ate Thanksgiving dinner with my parents, who had let the Republican hegemony of the 1980s drive them deep into an "indigenous peoples" phase, and served, along with dry, organically farmed turkey, a sampling of non-European grains, legumes, and roots, as well as the more traditional "maize on the cob," as they put it.

"Like the margarine commercial," Natalie remarked, pouring herself another glass of wine.

My father, as I have mentioned before, was testy that decade.

"Actually," he corrected her, "maize saved the Pilgrims long before that *actress* played a *squaw* in a commercial."

Faith blushed, not knowing Natalie's resilience. "Everything is delicious," she told my father. "The quinoa especially."

"So, Natalie," my mother asked, "what are you majoring in?"

"Poly Sci," she answered, "which is short for Political Science." She filled my wineglass, too, and started drinking it herself. "I find the political part interesting, anyway."

My father's eyes lit up momentarily. "How so?"

Natalie's face drew a blank, and she giggled.

"Leave her alone, Dad," Clive suggested.

"Well," Natalie started, "the classes are all really

big, so they don't take attendance, and they usually meet in the afternoon, so if I have to take an exam or something, I'm not hungover." She lifted the platter of corn. "Maize, anyone?"

The rest of the meal passed in a rare and uncomfortable silence. Faith and Clive, as it turned out, were in the process of breaking up, and their usually sparkling social skills had been dulled by sadness. My parents had received a notice in the mail that, once again, I would be placed on academic probation until my GPA climbed above a cumulative 2.0. I hadn't even known because my class attendance, that fall, had dipped to an all-time low, somewhere around ten percent, give or take a Human Sexuality class, which I attended as an unofficial auditor. That night, however, as I lay in my childhood bedroom with a snoring, unresponsive Natalie, I almost felt happy. I had come home an utter failure, with a girlfriend my parents hated, and an academic future that looked murky at best, especially when compared to my brother's. Even Clive, in the midst of his own despair, had taken me aside and asked me what the problem was at school. Could I be bored with the easy classwork? Did I ever think about, maybe, taking a semester off? Perfect Clive, if it had only been that simple. In all our years together he has never understood my need to tank the ship.

Natalie came to life, and rolled against my chest,

her head below my chin. I told her that I loved her more than anything else in the world: my family, myself, and maybe even God, too. With Natalie, making an impression was everything.

"Is that true?" she mumbled.

"I said it, didn't I?"

"You're sweet, but I have a boyfriend."

"Good night," I told her.

That giggle of hers, only sleepy this time. "Good night, Mike."

Before we left for school again I had a "kitchen talk" with my mother, named, in our family, for the location and importance of the conversation, and not because she felt especially at home around the machinery of domestic life—if anything her choice of venue was a private joke, a kind of thumb-to-the-nose at motherly convention. We hardly ever saw her in that room when we were growing up, except to heat a can of soup, or load a week's worth of dirty dishes into the mobile dishwasher, which hooked up to the kitchen faucet with a hose, and had a sticky wheel, meaning two of us were required to roll it in from the mudroom. Occasionally she used the wall phone, staring out the window at our neglected yard while she talked to a neighbor, or paced the linoleum while she listened to the romantic misadventures of her younger sister Charlotte, an elementary school teacher in Colorado. She laughed easily on the telephone, while in person she was rather stern, prone to be distracted by practical problems, like clogged gutters; one might call her *grounded*. Still, my mother is easily the smartest person I have ever met. By the time I was in college her study on the third floor had become a junk room, filled with obsolete technology: an Apple II computer, originally meant for keeping track of household expenses; an adding machine left over from a brief foray into accouting; an IBM PC 286 with a full software library, all pre-Windows, bought during the two semesters she spent in an MSW program at Simmons College. Nothing held her interest for longer than a year or two, and I have wondered, sometimes, if my mother might actually fit the profile of an underachiever. In the eyes of our neighborhood, perhaps; I prefer to think of her early accomplishments, and the fact that her marriage survived when so many others on Francis Street and beyond were failing, and don't forget the twins! Well, one of them is a productive member of society, and the other is a burden only on those closest to him. If Clive had trouble understanding my choices in life, my mother couldn't begin to conceive of them, and though she definitely loved me, and still does, according to the cards I receive on major holidays, I sometimes caught her looking at me with a guarded concern, as if I were a mysterious third cousin who had come to visit for a while, and not one half, give or take, of her progeny.

On the morning of our talk my mother hovered in

the doorway while I searched the kitchen for a decent breakfast. I grew up in a full-refrigerator household, yet there was never anything to eat, easily explained by the global array of condiments that lined the shelves—the refrigerator door must have weighed a hundred pounds, and slammed shut with the ringing of a belfry—while Baggies of fuzzy leftovers, never that tasty in the first place, far outnumbered the virgin groceries. Do I digress for any reason? Only to suggest that an early exposure to absence in the kitchen might explain my own austere taste in ice-box decoration. All right, so there's my income problem, too, but I must confess, the hunger/plenty paradox of my childhood kitchen still haunts me.

My mother crossed her arms and asked, "Do you want my help with anything?"

"Don't bother," I mumbled, searching the cereal library above the counter, which contained a rare 1974 edition of farina, among other antique items. I could feel her watching me, and I knew a serious question might be coming.

"Would you call yourself happy?"

I found a box of Cheerios from 1984, my freshman year in college, and poured it in a bowl before it turned to dust.

"I am now."

"Because we worry about you," she said. For our

"kitchen talk" my mother wore her usual L.L. Bean ensemble: a turtleneck, a chamois shirt, blue jeans, wool socks, Birkenstock sandals. A change in color from, say, maroon to periwinkle would have made no difference at all in her appearance. My mother, like many New Englanders, is practical to the point of being fashionless, which may account for the many costumes of my teenage years: preppie, jock, guido, new romantic, neopreppie, woodsman, Deadhead, panhandler, et cetera. "Your father and I both thought," my mother started in, "that by this time in your life you might be meeting your potential. You're sweet and capable, William, everybody knows it, but you just won't put your mind to anything. You're lazy. You have poor work habits. You surround yourself with screw-ups. Apparently you drink too much. You daydream, and when an opportunity comes your way to do something, I don't know, singular, you turn it down."

"I am not *sweet*," I said.

"Fine, you're a monster."

"What's your point?" I asked, trying to sink my ancient Cheerios, one by one, with the back of a spoon. Going stupid was the best way to trip her up, and when it came to the next step, stubborn silence, I could have taught classes at Harvard Extension. She looked anxious and a little saddened by my response.

"We want to know," she finally said, "what you

plan to do about your problem. You're an under-achiever, William, and I hope it doesn't hurt your feel-ings to hear me say so."

I pretended that her praise had wounded me.

"We know it isn't easy being Clive's twin brother. I'm sure there's a therapist you could see at school, or if you wanted, we could have you evaluated for a learning disorder. There's exciting diagnostics in the field today, and a test like that is nothing to be ashamed of."

I feigned another wound, and my mother changed the subject.

"Maybe college doesn't fit right now, and we could help you find a job."

A job? I honestly scowled. She could see that our talk was only making matters worse.

"Talk to me. Tell me what *you* think."

I heard unsteady footsteps upstairs, probably Nata-lie, who had trouble orienting herself in the morning. "Kevin?" she called out.

"I'd better go," I told my mother, dropping my spoon.

"Who's Kevin?" she asked disapprovingly.

I explained that it was Natalie's nickname for me, something to do with my resemblance, in a certain light, to Kevin Costner, the whitebread movie star. I was lying, of course.

"Kevin?" Natalie called from the top of the stairs. "What the fuck. Kevin?"

"I'm coming," I called.

"Can you bring me an aspirin?" Natalie whined.

"Sure, honey."

While I was at it I decided to lie again, and make a promise to my mother that I knew I wouldn't keep. "If, by the end of next semester, my average is lower than a 3.0, then I'll see a therapist."

"That's a fair response," she said.

"Don't nag me, though."

She drove a hard bargain, my mother. "No nagging, but only if I get a midterm update, independently verified."

"Deal," I said, bringing my cereal bowl to the sink. From there I would head upstairs and introduce myself to my girlfriend.

Looking back, now, I understand why my five years in college were perhaps the hardest that I have ever lived through. I was suffering from the same affliction that had troubled me from boyhood, only its symptoms, with time, had changed to meet my larger physiology: a young boy's tendency to underachieve had amplified to reach the far-flung regions of my mind and body, and when the call of failure sounded—how can I describe the exquisite torture of my secular little soul crying out to a greater God? Think of any shrill and futile sound, like a Sabine rape whistle—I went catatonic. I woke up every day at one o'clock, showered until two, made an afternoon class if I was lucky, and shuffled to the dining hall by six, where I took advantage of the steam tables repeatedly until one of the sweet cafeteria ladies, hairnet glistening in the fluorescent light, blue smock stained with gravy, showed me to the exit. I didn't know it then, but inside my problem skin I was going through a transformation, one that would unify my disappointing past and baffling present, my natural abilities and need to squander them, my perfect mirror-image and my imperfect self, so that I might, one morning—okay, afternoon—wake up from the long anxiety-dream of growing up and find myself arrived at the beginning of adulthood.

That Christmas, Clive traveled with his roommate back to the family plantation in Alabama, and I came home alone. Natalie and I had just broken up (I cried, she didn't) so she could spend more time with the brothers of Theta Delta Chi, and already I was seeing a freshman figure-skater named Nadine, who had overcome a serious hearing impairment to place fourth, nationally, at the Junior Olympics. "She means the *Special* Olympics," I used to joke in her presence. Nadine, an excellent lip-reader, was not afraid to hit me. I used to watch her practice at an ice rink across the stinking river, and though I was only a casual observer of the sport, it seemed to me that her talent and hard work could have taken her places if the people around her had been more professional. As it was, her "coach," a Zamboni driver by trade, choreographed her performances to whatever music he liked best, usually something off *Led Zeppelin II,* and when I knew her they were working on an "experimental" piece with a local call-in show on AM radio. Her hearing impairment made phone conversations impossible, and I had no friends to keep in touch with from the Boys' Prison (only traumatic memories), so I spent most of my month-long Christmas holiday staring at the ceiling, stricken with a case of the Romantic poet's *melancholia.* My whole life, it seemed, passed before me: first I was an infant crying out for something my sainted mother could never give me, then I was a dark and skinny boy, sick with childhood diseases, and finally a teenager, naive to the point of stupidity, clueless about where to start looking for my place in adult society. I hardly left my room. When my parents came in to see me, I asked them to leave. I grew pale and gaunt, and I didn't shower. At night I heard my parents outside my bedroom door, whispering about different ways to "intervene."

"If he has a mood disorder," my mother suggested, "it's highly treatable."

"Could it be the power lines?" my father asked. "He did spend a lot of time sitting by the window."

"Maybe he's withdrawing from substance abuse?"

"Have we checked the house for radon?"

"I can hear you," I told them.

Silence.

"Sorry," they said in unison.

At the beginning of week four an unfamiliar knock disturbed my reverie, and I sat up in bed, expecting some kind of psychoanalytic housecall, a quack from Brookline, maybe, with a cashmere turtleneck, and a serious prescription for something psychoactive. Instead, Faith Crick opened my door and stood there, smiling in.

"Hey there," she said, ignoring my appearance. "How's your break?"

I rubbed my greasy hair. "Harrowing."

She stayed in the doorway, tentative about coming inside. She had a suntan, and wore the purest white parka I had ever seen. "I was wondering if you wanted to go for a walk."

"Right now?" I asked stupidly.

"It's snowing."

"I guess I didn't notice."

"I'm leaving tomorrow. This is your only chance to see me."

"Did I miss Christmas?" I honestly wondered.

"Are you coming with me or not?"

"I'll need to clean up, I guess."

"You have ten minutes," she told me, "and then I spend this romantic winter moment by myself."

While I took a shower and shaved my eleven whiskers, Faith waited downstairs with my parents. Of course, I thought, they had asked her to come over and see me, but it turned out Faith had knocked on my door of her own volition.

"Don't freeze," my mother warned us, a little too brightly.

We bundled up in hats, scarves, vests, coats, and mittens, the Massachusetts spacesuit, and walked through freshly fallen powder down the length of Francis Street. The worst of the snow, or best, depending on how you look at it, had just stopped falling, and a few stray flakes still swirled underneath the street-lights, refusing to disappear. Faith shivered, newly unaccustomed to the climate, while I could have gone out that night in a T-shirt and shorts, as cold as it was upstate. We didn't talk much. Faith wrote her name in a snow-covered windshield. I wrote my own, crossed it out because I didn't like the way it looked, then spent the next five minutes cleaning the snow off the rest of the car, more to cover up my own mistake than out of altruism. Faith waited patiently, blowing in her mittens. "Almost done," I told her.

"Don't rush or anything," she said.

Once I had finished, we continued walking down to the Divinity School, darkened for vacation. We cleared off a spot on the cold stone steps and sat down in the glow of a security light, which buzzed and flickered faintly in the snowstorm silence.

"As neighborhoods go," I offered, "it could be worse."

"Other than the temperature," Faith said.

"Do you miss my brother?"

"Is this a test?"

"No."

"Yes."

"That's what I was thinking," I said.

"Do you?" she asked.

Funny, but I had never thought about it. Because Clive was my twin, I took him entirely for granted. I could go weeks, even months, without seeing him, and though, at the end, I knew I missed something, I would never have defined the emptiness as *him;* it seemed too personal, somehow, as if I really missed myself, and how could that be?

"Yes," I answered, "I do. I guess I miss him."

"I'll bet he misses both of us," she said, looking sad. "Do your parents know he's on an old plantation?"

"They told him he couldn't go, at first."

"What changed their minds?"

"He lied," I told her. "He claimed it was a stop on the Underground Railroad. After that they were *happy* to buy his plane ticket."

"And that was your idea, right?"

"Actually," I said, blushing in the cold.

"That's just the kind of thing that Clive would never think of. Don't get me wrong, William, he's doing just fine in the intelligence department, as well as every other one, but still . . ."

"He's the king," I said.

"But you have to admit," she went on, "his imagination is a little anemic."

"You think so?"

She blew in her mittens again. "His love letters were really sweet, but after a while I found them uninspired. I *loved* them when I was fourteen, and even when they started bugging me I was always happy to get them. Still, something was missing."

"Remind me never to write a Comp-Lit major," I said.

"You won't tell him?" she asked.

"Never, believe me."

We listened to the quiet city.

"I can't feel my ass anymore," I said.

Faith stood up. "Me neither. Here," she said, holding out a mittened hand, "let's go in."

We said good-night in the middle of the snowy street, and wished each other luck in school, in relationships, and with our families. That night was the first, last, and only time I would ever spend alone with Faith, but it made me think that all the years I had hovered on her periphery, hoping to get nearer, had come to something, if only that particular occasion which, by luck, had come about when I was at my lowest, and she, without knowing it, had been able to help me. As I have said before, the underachiever's life is a lonely one, devoid of sustaining warmth, and fundamental intimacy; this statelessness, if you will, can be the source of boundless happiness, a kind of transcendental bliss known only to the deepest American thinkers (Ralph Waldo Emerson, Henry David Thoreau, Tony Robbins); however, there are times when the burden of such a radical self-consciousness is too much to bear, even for an existential genius, and a few kind words from a friend, or unexpected good news in the mail, or an athletic one-night stand, make all the difference. Thank you, Faith, for choosing that pure white parka, and for believing in me.

I won't pretend that my difficult road, all of a sudden, became easy. Spring, on that barren little college campus, was sorority formal season, and since the Boys' Prison had frowned on the American prom (thankfully), I looked forward to accepting the invitations that were sure to begin appearing on the outside of my door, pinned there by lonely Greeks. On the way to my morning shower every afternoon I checked the hallway for envelopes, only to find the usual litter, and cruel graffiti. One by one my hallmates returned from class and discovered flowers and cryptic messages taped to their doors; even Wendell received three separate invitations in a flurry, and counting them became a competition in my all-boys' dorm, yet another masculine rite from which I was excluded. My hallmates left their invitations up, of course, and every time I left my room I walked a gauntlet of their popularity. Wendell basked in the glow of female attention, and started wearing English Leather. Now when he came back from class and found me still in bed he said, "I pity you, mate."

Finally, when the green carnations of the Phi Sigmas had wilted and dried, and the giant Tootsie Rolls of the tri-Deltas had all been plucked from their wrappers by our resident advisor, who had a permanent case of the munchies, I limped home from a violent game of Frisbee one night and found, propped against my door, a teddy bear with my name on it, the trademark of Sigma Delta Tau. I snatched the envelope from the animal's paws and tore it open. I had been invited, the photocopied page announced, to the seventh annual "Spring Spectacular," to be followed, the next morning, by a champagne breakfast and charity tag sale. My date's name? "To Be Determined." It was something, anyway, and when I burst into the room to tell Wendell, I found him eviscerating his own teddy with a pocket knife. He was inconsolable. His date for the evening was a notorious lesbian named Marcy Brown.

I have to admit, my memory of that first spring formal is a little spotty. I met my escort at a rushed ceremony in the sorority house, a basement apartment in Concrete Jungle. She was Wendell's height, at least;

when I asked her why she had invited me, she explained that her "big sister" had picked my name out of the freshman pig-book. I suspected that her blue satin dress was taller than me. I went straight to the bar, and stayed there until the social director herded us out of the building, by twos, into a yellow school bus. Seating on board was limited. To save space my date volunteered me to sit in her lap, and when I hesitated, her "big sister" pushed me in. Her perfume quickly overpowered me. Luckily I had stolen a bottle of vodka from the bar, which eased my discomfort, and as soon as we reached the Hyatt Regency I escaped to the men's room and threw up. From that point on I can only recall sipping deeply from a number of gin-and-tonics, the sight of Wendell's full-length duster being torn from his body, and watching a "dirty dancing" contest from underneath a banquet table, while my date tried to coax me out with a push broom. The next day Wendell swore he saw me dancing with my shirt off. All I know for sure is that for years afterward, whenever I heard the cheesy strains of "Sailing," I had to fight the urge to sprint.

I spent my sophomore year at school in the same drunken stupor, looking, I think, for another Natalie, and when I didn't find her I settled for a chaste communion with my favorite water bong. My "drug period" ended, during the fall of my second sophomore year, with a bad hallucination on a Ferris wheel, fol-

lowed by a week of flashbacks (clowns, spinning tea-
cups) that kept me confined to my dorm room. When I
finally sobered up, lucid for the first time in months, I
thought of my conversation in the snow with Faith
Crick, and how she believed that I had every right to
exist in the same charmed universe as my twin. I
hadn't seen her in a while, but word filtered back from
Francis Street that she always asked for me.

As sobriety began to work its magic I stopped re-
turning phone calls from my degenerate friends, and
started, for the first time, to attend my classes, sur-
prised, in the cases of Russian 101 and Modern Poetry,
that I had randomly chosen such interesting subjects at
registration. In the back row of poetry class, while the
accumulated fog of all that dope and keg beer slowly
cleared, I heard a chorus of voices like Augustine, *Take
it and read, take it and read,* and when I looked wildly
around the room to find the source, I met the mono-
cled gaze of Country Goodness Chicken and Wings
Professor of the Humanities (the English department's
only endowed chair) B. X. Hollis, darling of Canadian
critics, his handpicked classroom poised and quiet,
studying me. The radiators hissed. All of a sudden the
fog rolled in again. When I came back to consciousness
the classroom was empty. My notebook was open to a
page where I, or someone else, had written, *The hya-
cinth girl—pretty.* What was happening? Professor
Hollis watched me from the chalkboard, his arms

crossed; he lifted the monocle from his eye, wiped it with a handkerchief, and slipped it in its socket again. I fumbled with my notebook and tried to beat a hasty retreat.

"William," he said, stopping me, "is that right?"

"Yes, I think," I answered.

"Tell me, do you have something against reading aloud to the class?" He had raised an eyebrow for effect, which started twitching. Just then I remembered the rumors I had heard about his fraternity-style hazing fetish, bolstered by the paddle that hung from the wall in his office. Like all honorable perverts he liked to receive the punishment, apparently.

"No," I said.

"Good," he answered. "My office hours are on Thursdays, one o'clock sharp, and operate on a first-come, first-served basis."

"Thursdays," I repeated.

"Very well, then," he said, gathering his papers. "I hope to see you."

Needless to say I ignored his invitation, and after refusing, in the coming weeks, his persistent offers of gratis squash lessons, I finally agreed to a lunch of microwaved fish sticks at the faculty club, where, underneath the drape of a bright blue tarpaulin (renovations), he regaled me with stories of his hardscrabble youth in Alberta, which he spent in forced labor from the age of eight, turning candlesticks on a lathe in his father's workshop. "I keep a paddle in my office," he confessed once he felt comfortable that I was sympathetic and not a spy for the administration. "I made it myself, you know. Just like a pledge to a fraternity." He could barely contain his enthusiasm, and blushed. Over coffee and a healthy slice of Jell-O pie, the good professor Hollis offered me a position as his research assistant, and I accepted. I can say with some pride that he respected me too much to ask for my participation in his ritual punishment. Who would have guessed, just a year before, that I would end up collaborating—from a safe distance, mind you—with a scholar like B. X. Hollis on some ground-breaking research, even if, by the time of my departure from college two years later, our work remained largely unfinished, and would almost certainly end up discredited by the "spanking scandal"?

At our next class meeting I read aloud from "Old Possum's Book of Practical Cats," which Hollis thought of as Eliot's finest work after the little-known "Sweeney Erect"; when I finished "Mungojerrie and Rumpelteazer" the class let out a gasp, and Hollis asked me to continue all the way to "Mr. Mistoffelees." At last I had found a classroom where I felt comfortable with success. I was lucky to have met Hollis at a time when he could understand my problems, and offer wise, if unsettling, advice. If I had met him during the bright beginnings of his career, before his fraternity fetish got the better of him, my under-achieving scholarship would have meant nothing to him.

I will spare you the details of our lurid project—in broad strokes it involved Ezra Pound, William Butler Yeats, and a certain mahogany walking stick—and when I finally graduated from that insipid place I was happy to be done with it. In the meantime I had learned, firsthand, about the quack mentality behind the vast majority of academic scholarship, and I had met some interesting female research assistants in my travels to other, more legitimate, lending libraries. Sasha from Elmira, an upstate village of sexy hemo-philiacs, taught me erotic ways of giving blood. A budding feminist critic I met in Ithaca preferred anon-ymous sex in bathroom stalls. And my foray into pseudoscholarship appeased my parents back home, who knew little about the real Professor Hollis, only what they had read in Canadian journals, displayed prominently in the bookstores of Cambridge, home to the world's academic ephemera. An acknowledgment in the contributors' notes of *Poo-Bah* raised false hopes; my own pet project, while influenced by my mentor's questionable practices, turned out to be more personal in nature, and not exactly ripe for dissection at the Winnipeg MLA. I sought to get to the bottom of my underachieving with an examination of failure in life and letters, and in my free time, between beer crawls and running interference for Hollis, I managed to compile a composite sketch of, or more accurately, a list of characteristics shared by, notable underachievers in history, or at least the examples that I stumbled across over the course of my sporadic research. Don't ask me for citations! I admit a Western bias in the early sections, and an overall contempt for the lowest-common-denominator approach of "cultural studies." At the risk of redundancy, what follows is a small piece of my greater contribution to the record of human knowledge:

UNDERACHIEVING: A THEORY

1. Alone in an age of increasing competition and diminished possibilities, the underachiever, when faced with doing battle, will *forfeit* rather than draw blood in the modern arena. He is *powerless*, and *deliberately weak*.

2. The underachiever is *misanthropic by default*. He will use *negativity* as his greatest weapon, and reserves the right to criticize all that is exalted in both secular and religious society. He lives at a *calculated distance* from the mainstream, longing secretly to be included, while at the same time voicing his contempt for those who play by the rules, that is,

achievers of the garden variety, and especially his nemesis, the overachiever.

3. Rather than saying "Yes, yes" to life, the underachiever will say "No, thank you." If pressed, he will turn *belligerent*.

4. Underachievers are not to be confused with younger, slower brothers of southern presidents, like Billy Carter, and Roger Clinton *[a late addition— Ed.]*. These gentlemen do the best with whatever genetic leftovers they've been given, while the underachiever is entrusted with a master key to opportunity's home office, and misplaces it.

5. If the underachiever were a mixed drink, he would be a dry martini, one part *obscurity* (vermouth), three parts *unhappiness* (gin).

The list elaborates from there, all the way to #107 ("In Mesopotamian literature, the oldest in the world, the underachiever is represented by Enkidu—'the hunted mule, wild ass of the mountains, leopard of the open country' in *The Epic of Gilgamesh*—who gives up his satisfying 'primitive' lifestyle for the sexual charms of Shamhat, and the brotherhood of Gilgamesh. After killing Humbaba of the Pine Forest and the Bull of Heaven, Enkidu must be sacrificed in place of Gilgamesh to appease the gods. His death—by high

fever—is less tragic than pathetic. Among the Mesopotamian deities we can identify two underachievers,
Birdu, 'the pimple,' and Manungal, 'the snatcher,' both
from the Underworld, and known only for their epi-
thets").

I was disappointed when not a single journal editor
took an interest in my fledgling project; still, my research kept me busy, and provided a distraction from
the string of bad relationships that would carry me
through graduation. At the English department ceremony I received the Hollis Prize for independent
scholarship, an experience marred somewhat by the
spanking noises that erupted from the crowd, and the
fact that, due to a clerical error, I was never issued my
sky-blue cap and gown. Luckily I had failed to send
my family their invitations, and even if I had, I'm not
sure they would have made the trip upstate. My father
was going through his "public transportation" phase
then, and to reach that sickly corner of the landscape,
their only option would have been to take "the gray
dog."

During my senior spring I had fallen in love with
Christina, a theater major from Dallas, after seeing her
play Varya in *The Cherry Orchard* ("If only God could
help us!"), a production nearly ruined by the director,
a freshman prodigy who insisted that the actors wear
elaborate stage makeup, like the rock group Kiss. Noble, adopted Varya's face was marred by Ace Frehley's

silver thunderbolt. After graduation I followed Christina to San Francisco, having given her my half of a security deposit, and a few weeks to find a job and an apartment for us. When I called the number she had given me, friends in the Mission District, a strange man answered the phone in Vietnamese. He had never heard of Christina, or of an English dictionary, for that matter. I dialed nearly every sequence of those numbers from a pay phone just off Haight Street, and the closest that I came to Christina was a stoned woman who told me, "We have a Joey, a Bruce, and two Laurens. I'm Bruce." Then she erupted in a fit of giggling. I called my parents next, and as usual, they generously wired me some money, but not before they had extracted a little blood. I had to send them, in the next week or so, a payment plan for retiring my debt to them in full, a copy of my tax return that year, and an estimated monthly budget. Adulthood never felt as impossible as it did that June, looking for a job in an unfamiliar city, and an apartment that I could just afford, and the ex-girlfriend who had stolen all my graduation money. I found her two years later, in an all-female production of *Glengarry Glen Ross*, but her performance as Shelly Levene had been so riveting that I forgave her the loan. Who can resist a tragic, foulmouthed saleswoman?

I quickly rose to the occasion, thanks, for the most part, to San Francisco itself, a city deserving of all the hype, and the proud body politic that lives so happily within its limits. Of all the places I have lived, this city is the most unreal, and I mean that as a compliment. My first apartment was a shoe box in a neighborhood the realtor described, optimistically, as Nob Hill, meaning the seedy Tenderloin, where my next door neighbor was an amateur pornographer from Russia. He was an angry man, and welcomed me to the neighborhood with a right hook to the jaw. After a short time, though, I came to feel at home among the junkies, mumblers, and chronic masturbators, even knew a few of them by name, until a brutal mugging by a group of children sent me packing, low on money, bundle on my back, to an apartment share on lower Haight.

What can I say about the city I found during those first, aimless weeks? I had never seen streets so wide; each crosswalk approximated, it seemed, the very Western frontier, and the low-slung buildings let a clear blue sky, or fog, or sudden altocumulus apparitions, claim dominion over all, especially on top of the famous hills, where the mansions of Pacific Heights looked more like tree houses, the handiwork of wealthy children with early training in Beaux Arts architecture. At every curb I had to summon the courage to cross the street, and I came to see that on the East Coast, our narrow streets and skinny houses spoke volumes about our frightened sensibility. My heart beat faster, literally, at every corner. The people I met were friendly, spontaneous, and healthy, if a little stupid, but, hey—they had found a place where happiness, the pure, unbridled kind that no one knew in Massachusetts, was an actual, concrete possibility, and leave it to me, for once the reluctant underachiever, to show up famished and spoil the sourdough party.

A short list of my many service-sector jobs that first year follows, with some deletions for the sake of continuity: I rolled burritos in the Mission, steamed milk and made espresso in North Beach, shelved books on upper Haight, and, last but not least, folded muscle shirts on Castro Street, under the watchful eye of a sleazy manager named Ralphie, who wore an eye patch for no real reason and, for a while, required the same of every employee in his gift shop. After a week of double shifts at Body Beautiful, my left eye became oversensitive to sunlight, and swelled and teared whenever I went outside, as if I had a permanent case of conjunctivitis. A brief eye-drop addiction followed, until I bought a pair of aviator sunglasses, my "trademark" look for a while, but I lost them overboard during a ferry trip to Alcatraz, the perfect date, I thought, ruined by my clumsiness, because from that moment on, apparently, my ponytailed companion thought I was crying.

Clive had spent an entire year traveling abroad, and came back that fall to study law at Stanford, in nearby

Palo Alto. We had dinner every few weeks at a little Italian place called Michelangelo, and he told me stories about his travels, the one year, in all our lives, when we had truly been separated. While he described the Florentine beauty who had offered him a ride on her Vespa, or the troubled daughter of a Greek industrialist he had met on the boat to Crete, my mind wandered to the bigger-ticket items on the menu. He looked great, as always, and I looked like a cabdriver: I was trying to grow my hair out, and had gone so far as to start a dreadlock on one side, which looked like the seedpod for a little alien, and attracted lice, not to mention my eleven whiskers, which I held together with a rubber band in some foolish dream of a beard. Clive never said a word about my further experiments in ugliness, and always paid for dinner with his gold card. He was as generous and kind as I was skeptical and weak.

Other than Clive, and the odd, underachieving co-worker whom I actually liked, and the bizarre collection of roommates I was gathering (Cyrus the junkie, Martha the auto mechanic, Orla who did nothing), I spent most of my time with a poet I had fallen in with named Victor, who was easy company, and just as hard up for a girlfriend, so he was willing to spend his precious hours away from a different, though equally degrading, service-sector job in search of women.

Victor was the first real poet I had ever met. He

wore the same dark green turtleneck every day, and small round glasses. In addition to looking for a girlfriend, Victor was in the process of inventing his own language, which I found exciting. We often took the bus to Marina Boulevard and walked along the promenade, smiling at the joggers as they ran by. When Victor grew short of breath and started coughing, the unfortunate side effect of his pack-a-day clove cigarette habit, we sat down on a park bench and looked out at the bay, at fog slowly enveloping Alcatraz Island, or filtering through the wires of the Golden Gate bridge like a net, rolling down the hills of Sausalito to the water.

"I hear Seattle is getting cool," Victor would say, his next clove already lit.

"Is it?" I asked.

"You like coffee?"

"Not after that café job. I drank, like, twenty cups a day. Talk about wired."

"I call it *kefta*," Victor told me, "which sounds better, don't you think?" A pretty jogger was approaching, and Victor blew clove smoke in her path, intentionally. It was his way of getting them to stop.

"I thought *kefta* was already taken."

"Yeah?"

"For kabobs. *Kefta* kabobs, ever heard of those?"

The jogger steered away from us, holding her

breath as she passed, and Victor tossed his clove butt in her wake. "You think I care about that shit?"

Life can be cruel to poets, especially in a city already filled with them, and I admired Victor for his persistence. He sent his poems out to small magazines, which always returned them with a photocopied rejection slip, and sat through countless readings at bookstores and coffeehouses in the hope that someone, after a while, might recognize him as a "scenester," strike up a conversation, and invite him to read his work— this was before the explosion of poetry slams and open-mike nights made working poets out of everyone who could afford to pay a cover charge. He was forever making copies of the same five poems and handing them out to strangers, who either gave him blanket encouragement, or were highly critical of his obscurantist experiments. Finally, Victor's tireless self-promotion paid off, and he was offered a Sunday-morning reading slot at a sushi bar on Divisadero. In order to stay and watch him, I had to order a California roll and a pitcher of sake, and I listened to him pour out his soul to a mostly empty restaurant. Besides Victor himself, no one had a clue about what was on his mind. *I am soo*, he finished, *plate me, nix wannabe.* I clapped wildly. Victor walked back to the sushi bar and sat down beside me, a little shaky. "Waitress," I said, "get this man some *tekka.*"

"What did you think?" he asked, trying to clean his glasses with his filthy turtleneck. "Was I great, or what?"

"Sublime."

"When I was up there," he said, "I could tell the ladies were really digging me. I'm a *magnet.*"

To be honest, I hadn't noticed any "ladies" in the restaurant. "There was me," I said, "the Vietnam veteran guy in the corner, and the deliveryman, the one with the bags of rice."

"The girl with the tray, stupid."

"She's a waitress, Victor. She was trying to take your order."

"Well," he said, mixing wasabi into his soy sauce, "she was looking at me up there. I haven't lost it."

I stopped hanging out with Victor after he found the woman of his dreams, a Vietnamese teenager, pretty in a lost sort of way, who worked fifty hours a week in a sweatshop to pay off her smuggling ransom, and spoke very little English. He believed that he was liberating her, heroically, from the clutches of a crime triad. My own love life offered no such adventures, just more low-grade heartbreak, the worst kind, and a run-in or two with crabs. Clive had tried to set me up with a few law students who, as he put it, wanted to "take a walk on the wild side," but when they found no heroin or motorcycles on my resume, they gave me the proverbial Heisman. And in a strange twist, counterintuitive to everything I had been taught about self-reliance, the longer I stayed in San Francisco working full-time jobs, the worse they got, as if I were slipping down a ladder someone cruel had greased: frying fish at a restaurant on the Wharf; "pulling waste" at an office building after hours (work too low, even, for a full-time janitor); handing flyers out to tourists at Golden Gate Park, which was illegal, apparently, judging by the fines. The truth is, I found freedom in my misery: having disappointed every expectation that my parents held for me, I had finally been cast out of their constructive thoughts, written off for good; they no longer derided me for my lack of ambition every time we spoke, and even my mother, who did not give up easily, had exhausted her capacity to needle me. In short they had forgotten me, the underachiever's secret wish. There was no one left to disappoint because my life was truly lonely, and I had abandoned my own career expectations long before the fryer clogged my pores, the trash bags began disintegrating in my grasp, the handbills advertised not clearance sales and breakfast specials, but my s——tty life. I had managed to become, despite the privilege of my upbringing, a member of the "unwashed masses," the very group my parents so revered, romanticized, and condescended to from their liberal distance, tucked away in the crooked

eaves of their Victorian mansion. My family had endless sympathy for other people, as long as they would
never, in the course of *real* life, see them.

In retrospect my finest hour in San Francisco came
when I was fired from a job I genuinely liked—flower
delivery—for leaving the van running outside a
painted lady on Beulah Street, and handing an orchid
over to a man obsessed with maps, judging by his taste
in hallway decorations, while teenagers, tattooed and
pierced, drove off with the rest of my afternoon deliv-
eries. I took a bus back to the florist shop, run by
Cossack tyrants, and broke the news as gently as I
could, trying not to laugh.

"Your people," I added, "have an ugly history."

Ostap, the patriarch, led me to the door by my left
ear, the ringing one. We brushed past azaleas yet to
bloom, and a bucket of yesterday's baby's breath. I
could see now that he hated me, and he always had,
and any civil contact we had shared before had taken
place out of sheer necessity, a temporary flowering of
his dark and undernourished heart-blossom. I was
nothing to him, and soon he would forget me. What
freedom! I spent the rest of the afternoon walking
around in a daze, in love with my invisibility.

But even at the height of my ascendance, Clive insisted on trying his best to help me. As far as he was
concerned, I had extended my adolescence for long
enough, beyond the limits, even, of a normal under-

achiever, and the time was fast approaching when I would have to try and make a reasonable life for myself, not this loser's parody that I was living, but a real one, with responsibility, and relationships, and tax deductions—in short, terrifying conventional risks. Clive's biweekly visit from Palo Alto was poorly timed, and I dreaded hearing his dull, practical advice about how to change my circumstances.

We met at the Stinking Rose, just the kind of quirky tourist spot he liked, a garlic restaurant on Columbus Avenue near City Lights, the spiffed-up beatnik bookstore where we bought presents for our father to feed his growing nostalgia for the Revolution. We discussed my future over pungent roasted garlic bulbs and crusty bread, to start. Already people had begun to stare; we were a perfect mismatched pair that night, one twin a clean-cut future lawyer, the other a godfather of grunge, and as usual, I was ravenous.

"Save some room," Clive advised me first, "you'll fill up on that sourdough."

I ripped off another piece, ignoring him.

Clive looked around the room, decorated with garlic braids and empty bottles of Chianti. "No werewolves allowed, I guess."

"Vampires, you mean."

"No, it's werewolves."

"Whatever." I handed our waitress the empty bread basket. "More, please."

Clive started in. "You know, I was thinking, now might be a good time for you to go back to school. You don't have to start with rocket science, maybe something practical. It wouldn't hurt to pick up some marketable skills."

"By practical, do you mean technical college?"

"Maybe."

That pissed me off. "Jesus, Clive, I'm not retarded or something. I'm in a rut right now, I'll admit that, but let's not forget the tests that prove, beyond the shadow of a doubt, that I'm smarter than you."

He lowered his eyes, embarrassed for me. "Fine, just keep it down."

By the time my chicken roasted with forty garlic bulbs arrived, I was full. Clive had paced himself, and while he ate his dinner happily, he gave me advice about getting into law school, if that was closer to what I had in mind. Then he asked if I was finished with my chicken, switched plates with me, and kept talking. After a while I interrupted him and said, "I get the picture, all right?"

"Then maybe law school isn't right for you," he tried. "Maybe you could take some science classes, and think about applying to medical school."

"But the blood," I said, wincing.

"All right," Clive said, trying again, "why don't you go to art school, and learn how to take photographs? You used to love taking pictures, didn't you?"

"I'm against photography," I claimed. "It's a despicable, soul-stealing art."

Clive put his fork down. "I'm out, then."

"Nice try," I told him.

He motioned for the check. "You're a real bastard sometimes, William."

I wish I could say that my next big life-decision, joining a mysterious cult in the Haight-Ashbury neighborhood, resulted from a conscious choice to multiply my invisibility by another degree. Like all experiences that have marked me, I bumped into it by accident, or more accurately, in this case, I was recruited: searching through the grass one day at Golden Gate Park for an errant Hacky Sack, I noticed that a striking woman, shirtless underneath her overalls, had trained her eye on me. She had close-cropped hair, intense dark eyes, and the long, thin arms of a high-school basketball player. I cannot describe the depth of her gaze, only that it promised something intimate, and recognized, I thought, my untapped potential for genuine feeling, all of which I gathered in the few seconds that it took her to approach me on the grass, bend over gracefully, pick up my Hacky Sack, and hold it out like an angel of lost objects, hope for my late-century dreams.

"Is this yours?" she asked.

"I think so," I answered, dumbfounded. "Bad kick, I guess."

"It happens."

"Do you sack?"

I couldn't believe my idiotic question, but she in-
dulged me in a short demonstration, and soon we were
sacking in a secluded corner of the Botanical Gardens,
a juniper bush between us for greater difficulty.

"Are you from here?" I asked.

"No," she answered, hopping for an errant shot,
"I'm from Ohio." She returned the Hacky Sack with a
deceptive underspin, which flatfooted me.

"You?"

"I'm from back East."

"Don't tell me, New Jersey?"

"Nope."

"Massachusetts, or whatever?"

As if she knew me!

"Cambridge," I said, launching a shot above her
head and into the Biblical Garden, flowering plants
from Asia Minor around the time of historical Jesus.
She looked lovely in her overalls, surrounded by
Papaver Rhoeas, orange field poppy.

"Sorry."

She told me her name was Frida, but once I had
followed her into the cult I knew her only by her
appointed alias, the Peacemaker. My name? The
Wanderer, as if I had any other skills to contribute.
We also had among our ranks a Painter, Cook, Chambermaid, Thief, and, author of all our functions within

the cult's membership, a Leader. After Clive engineered my "escape" I would discover, through a little research, that this aimless organization was just a local rip-off of the Finders, an espionage cult in Washington, D.C., but at the beginning I found their secrecy and illogic fascinating, if not romantic. And the Peacemaker had a hold on my imagination like a lover, even if our relationship, if you will allow me, diary, to use an inappropriate word, amounted to a version of enslavement where I followed her, having nothing in my life and nowhere else to go, into a rundown commune on a forgotten block of Fillmore, where I was asked to perform a series of tasks designed to test my willingness to bend, if not break, according to my Leader's will, all in exchange for a glimpse of her bright smudge of a morning face across the breakfast table; or the promise, once I had been welcomed into the high order, of a shared mission to Cal Foods, where I would stand lookout as she shoplifted the makings of our Leader's only dietary intake, pizza bagels; or, sweet dream, a backrub—it happened only once, but that was enough to sustain me through six months of servitude and psychological trauma: the Peacemaker came to me in my flea-infested room, while the Painter, my roommate, was out on a "landscape mission." She knocked, invited herself in, and sweetly, even shyly, I mistook, peeled off my purple wandering shirt, and began to knead together, with sharp knuckles, and tender fingers, long-neglected muscle, bone, and skin, until my perpetually afflicted body, so fickle as to make me feel unreal, joined together with my mind in a kind of post-Cartesian, master-and-servant, contemporary realism. "Wow," I whispered, and she told me, "Don't worry, the Leader isn't here." Then she launched into a prepared speech about how much the Leader appreciated my presence in the commune. Every night we were summoned into his chambers, one by one, to brief him on our activities. He never seemed particularly thrilled to see me, perhaps because I followed the Peacemaker in rank, and there was a certain, shall we say, odor in his bedroom that spoke of humid encounter—not to mention the disorder of his bedsheets.

"He sees great things for you," she confided, and I knew it was a script. Still, I sank deeper into new corporeal bliss.

"A little to the left, please."

"Right there?" she asked, working magic.

"Yes, that's it."

"You have strong shoulders," she lied.

I had to ruin everything and make a clumsy move, but by then it didn't matter. She had touched me. While the afternoon fog rolled in my broken window, Frida's nursemaid routine injected me with a small measure of her inner peace. In her care, I was happy to be sick.

After the initial blush of the Leader's mind control wore off I realized I had joined a cult of losers. The Leader suffered from a lack of height, chronic asthma, and a delusional imagination that had him, among other things, leaving San Francisco at any minute to advise a new revolutionary movement taking shape in Mexico, the Zapatistas. Basically, he didn't want to lift a finger, and filled his decaying house, an inheritance from a kindly grandmother, with lost souls who wanted to belong to something larger than themselves and, in return, didn't mind performing a little house-work. Some of this I learned in a newspaper article about the Leader's arrest for corrupting a minor two years earlier that the Chambermaid, a former crossing guard, slipped underneath my pillow (sadly, she had a crush). Her disloyalty was a symptom of the disappointment we all shared in the Leader's skills. He looked the part—long, unkempt hair; a scholar's glasses; safari shirts and faded jeans—but, shrunk down to three-fifths scale, something vital in his image was missing.

From what I understand, many successful dictators have been short in stature, and have suffered from petty ailments and unusual personality quirks. They have ruled, instead, by force of will, and an enlarged sense of their own value. Our Leader had a passive ruling style, considering he spent the greater part of every day in bed, and his habit of interrupting motivational speeches to suck on his inhaler, or assigning twelve-hour shifts at the toaster oven to prepare his pizza bagels, could only serve to turn the membership against him. The Cook, who had taken some nutrition courses at San Francisco State, was appalled by the Leader's diet. He had a long black beard that he sometimes braided, and was the kind of man who ground his coffee beans by hand. On weekends he attended Rainbow Gatherings. The Thief, not a genius, exactly, quickly ran out of places in the neighborhood where he could steal groceries undetected, and rather than wasting his time by driving all over the city, he took to buying them with money from his trust fund. We suspected nothing at the time: his room at the commune was just as bare as the rest, and his surfer persona led us to believe that he had been raised by hippies on Muir Beach. It was all a ruse, however, and again I have the Chambermaid to thank for bringing his true nature to my attention—after he spent a suspicious weekend reconnaissance mission with the Peacemaker, the Chambermaid presented me with a credit-card slip for the Point Reyes Seashore Lodge in Olema, the most romantic spot, perhaps, in all of Marin County. The Thief had a net worth in the low six figures, by the Chambermaid's best estimate, and the Peacemaker, tired of her squalid surroundings, couldn't resist his promises of luxury. Our Leader was too out of it to notice her indiscretion. She continued to perform her functions dutifully, but not without a toll: late one night, on a trip downstairs to pilfer an extra ration of Triscuits, I saw her slip out of the Leader's chambers in a nightshirt, pass the Thief's door without a nod, and close herself in the communal bathroom. The sound of running bathwater mingled with her muffled sobs. I felt for her.

The only satisfied member of the commune was the Painter (an ex-schoolteacher from dairy country in Vermont), who had given up on education to spend his days outdoors with a straw hat, paint palette, and compact aluminum easel, capturing the many faces of that pastel city on squares of cardboard, and scraps of wood, which he hung on every available vertical surface in the house, until the commune felt less like a place to live than a knickknack shop and "art gallery" for tourists. His style can only be described as Happy Edward Hopper. "Wet paint!" he used to yell on his way in from a mission, and slap the picture up wherever there was room, before he grabbed our daily copy of the newspaper that the Thief (allegedly) had clipped, and retired to the toilet. No one liked his work. He was completely without talent, utterly driven, and he berated us, quite frequently, for brushing up against his freshest pieces, a problem that resulted in hours of touch-up work for him and, for me, ruined wandering shirts. As his roommate I endured his oily smell, paint prints on my books and furniture, snoring at the Who

level, and his disinterest in gossip about the commune.
How I respected him! I have often thought that if my
cult experience provided me with anything to learn, it
would be through his example; never before had I seen
such blindness to the kinds of compromise that ruled
his life, and a willingness to sacrifice his circumstances
for a hopeless passion, doomed from the beginning.

Throughout my time in the commune I kept on
dropping hints about my plight to Clive in Palo Alto,
veiled references to Charles Manson and the Tate
murder, allusions to the abduction of Patty Hearst, and
to his credit (once again) he was responsible for my
liberation when the Peacemaker's promises for a
bright future in her chambers no longer meant anything to me, nearly a year after she had chosen me for
their job opening. Besides, I owed Clive a lot of
money. Wandering aimlessly doesn't pay much of a
salary.

Perhaps I have committed a sin of omission: I spoke
to Clive often by telephone, saw him weekly, and during periods when long-distance service at the commune had been disconnected, or our parents had
changed the PIN to their calling card again, we ex-
changed postcards and letters in our strange hiero-
glyphic script that no one else could decipher, such was
our need to communicate. If you do not have a twin
yourself, you will not understand the intense-yet-
distant nature of the adult relationship, which allows

each twin to establish his or her independence while, at the same time, keeping the other within near-umbilical reach. Clive had grown used to my rogues' gallery of roommates, and once he got over the novelty of asking for "the Wanderer" when he called the commune, my living arrangements must have seemed no different from the other flophouses where I had taken shelter from society's conventions.

One afternoon in early September, or maybe it was May, I had grown tired of wandering the hills of Ashbury in a purple T-shirt for no reason, so I went back to the commune early in the hope of finding the Painter out creating, and our room in a nap-friendly state. Not only was my roommate gone but the entire house, it seemed, was empty. A note on the kitchen table read: *Dinner at 7:00—rice, beans, escarole, misc. leftovers. Any complaints, take it up with the Peacemaker. I'm doing my best under poor circumstances. The Cook.* I decided to make myself a pizza bagel— strictly forbidden—with ingredients from the Leader's shelf in the refrigerator. I remember that I had just dripped sauce on my wandering shirt, and had decided, instantly, not to clean it, when a force attacked me from behind, twisting me into a painful headlock, and dragged me across the kitchen floor to our "secret" entrance, out the door, and down the steps into our scrubby yard, all with an economy and tenderness that should have been familiar.

"I'm sorry about the bagel," I gasped, "but there was nothing else to eat."

"Pipe down," Clive told me. "Once we're through the hedge, I'm letting go. Then we take off running. Just follow me, okay?"

"Clive!"

"Quiet!"

I was moved that my brother had come down from Palo Alto just to rescue me; still, his headlock brought back a lot of memories, none pleasant, and I started struggling to free myself. "Let go!" I pleaded.

"Not a chance," Clive answered, clamping down harder on my neck. "So they brainwashed you, right?"

"I don't think so."

"You know who you are, and everything?"

"Yes," I said, "just let go. Please." Clive did the right thing and dragged me through the hedge to safety before he let me out of his grip. We gasped for air together. I fell to my knees and touched the blessed earth. Our struggle had torn my T-shirt in a couple of places, and even though commune policy dictated that I would have to buy a new one, I didn't care.

"Since when did you wear purple?" he said.

"Shut up, Clive."

"Hey, I just saved your life."

"Nice try, but I was fine in there."

"You said you were a hostage."

"Did I?"

There, in a stranger's herb garden, he presented me with the last letter I had written him, drawing my attention to a paragraph that began: *I am afraid that if I try to leave, there might be consequences. No one has overtly threatened me. But the Leader is always talking about desertion, and his belief that "no justice is swift enough" to punish traitors to the commune. How's everything at school?*

I apologized to Clive, and explained that I had spent a long day on my feet, and might have been stretching the truth.

"Does this mean," Clive asked, "you actually *chose* to live here?"

"Not exactly," I answered.

"Really," he said, mulling the whole thing over.

I looked back at my bedroom window on the second floor of the commune, and saw that it was dark; just days before I had hung a piece of cardboard to fill the broken windowpane, and already the Painter had decorated the inside with a likeness of Ghirardelli Square. Over time I had grown to despise his industry. The Chambermaid, tired of cleaning up his mess, had recently organized a meeting to discuss his expulsion from the membership. Now that I had been sprung dramatically by my brother, how could I return to life in that failure of a cult? I kind of wanted my futon, though, and with Clive's help, I estimated, we could have my things outside in fifteen minutes.

"Where's your car parked?"

"Around the corner," Clive said, growing warier by the second. "Why?"

"I think I need a break from city life."

"Oh, no."

"One month," I promised, "maybe two at the most. Right now Palo Alto's just about my speed."

We survived this unfortunate misunderstanding, just as we have survived all my other episodes of blatant underachieving, and if I have been put on this earth to teach my better twin a lesson about the perils of compassion, for once he has failed to learn something. Even when my parents, who since 1964 have thrown away their collective vote like clockwork on losing presidential candidates, somehow managed to foresee the bitter end of my latest Master Plan, Clive always gave me the benefit of the doubt. I believe this is his only fault, although my ambition for this diary has never been to pick and prod my brother's character until it bleeds; our family is blessedly free of memoirists, thank you, along with clinical psychologists, social workers, and organ thieves.

How do you feel about your brother?

I would have had an easier time if Clive's weaknesses hadn't always been so admirable, and mine hadn't proved so selfish in comparison. But now I am at peace with our differences.

How do you feel about your father?

He was an engineer before he retired to the refuge of his study, trained in the specifics of sound, noise, and vibrational control, an experimental field with a myriad of real-world applications, like designing the perfect "hush" for a Quaker meetinghouse, or the "silence" in the reading room of a public library. His work was entirely invisible, and I wonder if the unsung nature of his profession, together with his marginal place in the political spectrum, haven't combined, in some way, to poison his spirit, nothing fatal, mind you, but enough of a dose to weaken his resistance to nostalgia and anachronism. Lately he has taken to wearing earplugs around the house and complaining to my mother when he senses a change in barometric pressure. In his old age he will look more and more Arthur Fiedleresque, if you know what I mean. He spends his days alone, listening to a handheld weather radio at full volume.

How do you feel about your mother?

I respect, honor, and cherish her place in my underachiever's world, even if I know that my way of life will always be a mystery to her, and every choice I make is subject, in her eyes, to a judgment based on what I might have been ideally, as if my resistance to reaching my utmost potential were just a phase in my development, and not a lifelong project in and of itself. Together and separately our parents instilled in their twins a fierce, enabling independence that would have us sacrifice the short-term gain for the progress of deeply held beliefs, regardless of parental pressure, brotherly guilt, or majority opinion. Clive is the upside of this bargain, and I am the downside. So be it.

In the fifth lecture of his *General Introduction to Psychoanalysis,* "Difficulties and Preliminary Approaches to the Subject," about sleep and dreaming, Dr. Sigmund Freud writes:

> Our relationship to the world which we enter so unwillingly seems to be endurable only with intermission; hence we withdraw again periodically into the condition prior to our entrance into the world: that is to say, into intrauterine existence. At any rate, we try to bring about quite similar conditions—warmth, darkness, and absence of stimulus—characteristic of that state. . . . It looks as if we grown-ups do not belong wholly to the world, but only two thirds; one third of us has never been born at all.

I have read this passage over many times, trying to determine if, indeed, this thesis can extend into my waking life, explaining my predisposition to outright failure, or at the very least, a kind of half-born existence where the better part of me is sleeping in my amniotic bed. I am an identical twin, one of two broth-

ers born from the same mutant egg; during my in-
trauterine existence, then, I had company, someone to
evolve with all the way from fish, to amphibian, to
human infant. We were different then just as we are
now, but all the same we share genetics, and our mirror images, though not strictly identical throughout
our childhood, were pretty close, even to the trained
eyes of our parents. Back in utero again: When I heard
my brother's heartbeat mingle with my own, what did
I think it meant? When I felt his knee against my
elbow, or the soft touch of his fingers against my
cheek, how could I have known that he would turn out
almost just like me, almost completely different? And
what has it meant to have another version of myself
who walks in many of the same places, seeing things
that I will never see? Feeling sensations that are all his
own? Keeping secrets from me? I respect Clive's right
to be a high achiever, just as I defend my own to fail
miserably; after all, the two of us were born, on the
same day, roughly equal in every category, a fact our
parents, typically, reminded themselves of whenever
Clive surpassed me in something new. The truth is,
even when I was at my weakest, Clive never considered himself to be my better half, living, as he does,
within the same thin skin that barely covers my neurotic tendency to belittle everything I touch, or feel, or
believe in. Also typical: I thought he felt sorry for me.

I have one more story to relate from my book of

bad memories, before I leave this diary for good, and start the next phase of my life, to gather in a larger volume (maybe). The place: New York City, a beautiful, decaying machine with many leaks, gaping holes, and moving parts, all of them hypnotic, and some dangerous to bystanders. The time: the recent past, some time after San Francisco, and before I packed my things and lit out for another pasture somewhere bleak. The characters: me, well known to you by now as a shameless dupe, and something of a doormat, romantically speaking; I'll call her Krista, a Swedish waitress with an expired student visa, pale blue eyes, and a hankering for an official, INS-approved green card; her "cousin" Bjorn, a drummer. Sound intriguing? The angle here is so obvious, the situation so irresistibly hopeless, that I will have to fall in love with her, out of my underachiever's moral duty. But will I go through with the wedding? You bet, in a quiet ceremony at City Hall, presided over by a justice of the peace in giant postoperative cataract sunglasses, with the bearded "cousin" of the bride, Bjorn, as sworn witness. Afterward, the happy couple and their wedding party (Bjorn, that is) walk across the Brooklyn Bridge, dodging bicycles in both directions, and the newlyweds share a quick kiss in the shadows underneath one of the granite towers. Bjorn rubs his beard unhappily beside them. "Wait," the wife suddenly remembers, "I have to bring my cousin to the train station. Can I meet you back at home, perhaps, before he's late?" One look from such tender eyes is all the husband needs, and he shakes his new cousin's hand, bowing good-bye (it's a foreign custom), and wishing the immigrants luck. "I'll have dinner on the table around eight," he tells his wife. "I bought a little surprise. Herring." Predictions, anyone? Will the gullible husband ever see his wife again? Once more, regrettably, for a mercy coupling, and then she is off with her "cousin" on a family trip, while her husband pines away for her in Harlem. Another hope diminished. Another chapter of my diary begun, slaved over, and finished.

Since then I have gone on to live other, similar lives in different places, unified by the particularities of my neurotic disease. My life is not great art, nor is it entertainment, nor is it the celebrity news and gossip that pervades our culture in this, the "age of information." With this diary I have tried to come to terms with my imperfect nature as quietly as one can, and still speak of it, without confusing my peculiar quirks with virtue, and proclaiming them aloud for everyone to hear, as if I were something more than what I am, an underachiever.

What, I ask, if my life had gone differently from the very beginning? If instead of finding sickness, loneliness, and trouble from an early age I had passed through life like a force of good nature, like my better twin? What if I had *wowed* them at the children's

Hort, excelled my way through grammar school and
the Boys' Prison to the college of my choice and, later,
chosen the profession that would have made my liberal parents proudest of all—politics? What if Faith
Crick had ignored my brother and had fallen in love
with me instead? I have no interest in the compromises of success. I wouldn't trade my uneventful
life for any shining consolation on the marketplace, for
any faithful love to spend her life with me, or adorable
child to smile up at me and say, *Dad?* From my calculated distance (see "Underachieving: A Theory"), I
have come to recognize the beauty at the heart of everything I've missed. I have learned a reverence for
broken things, for our fragile bodies, and for the tran-
sitory nature of human relationships. Like a modern-
day ascetic, I will call this beauty *holiness.* I can see it
in the hallways of the house where I grew up in Cambridge, Massachusetts, in my disappointed parents'
lives and in my successful brother's, too, certainly
when I remember my wife (wherever she is); and on
the upstate campus where I skipped so many classes,
draped like a shroud over the shoulders of the tenured
faculty; and in the eyes of Natalie, my sweet, liquor-
addled ex-girlfriend, who still managed to graduate a
year before I did; and in the lives of my fellow wanderers in San Francisco, looking for the promised land
in cult membership. Name all the people I have
known and not one soul is finished, we are a litany of

criminals-against-perfection that will last forever, or at least until our time on this spinning puddle comes to an end. Are you still listening, or have I lost you to private thoughts of joy and misery? No matter, and if I leave this diary, too, unfinished, then I have captured something of the shape to my experience, second fiddle that I am, wordy malcontent, hopeful liar, preacher of a small and useless gospel truth.